DEC   2010

gonefromthesewoods

gonefromthesewoods

DONNY BAILEY SEAGRAVES

Delacorte Press

Copyright © 2009 by Donny Bailey Seagraves

Published by Delacorte Press, an imprint of Random House
Children's Books, a division of Random House, Inc., New York

Delacorte Press is a registered trademark and the colophon
is a trademark of Random House, Inc.

www.randomhouse.com/kids

Educators and librarians, for a variety of teaching tools, visit us at
www.randomhouse.com/teachers

Library of Congress Cataloging-in-Publication Data
Seagraves, Donny Bailey.
Gone from these woods / Donny Bailey Seagraves. — 1st ed.
p. cm.
Summary: Feeling like a monstrous villain in one of his comic books,
eleven-year-old Daniel tries to cope with the guilt after accidentally killing
his beloved uncle while hunting in the woods of North Georgia.
ISBN 978-0-385-73629-9 (hardcover)
ISBN 978-0-385-90599-2 (library binding)
ISBN 978-0-375-89372-8 (e-book)
[1. Guilt—Fiction. 2. Death—Fiction. 3. Family problems—Fiction.
4. Georgia—Fiction.] I. Title.
PZ7.S43774Go 2009
[Fic]—dc22
2008028467

The text of this book is set in 12-point Goudy.

Book design by Kenny Holcomb

Printed in the United States of America

10 9 8 7 6 5 4 3 2

First Edition

This book is dedicated to the memory of my second-grade teacher,
Dycie Hancock Schneider. Also to the memories of her first husband,
William Campbell; her nephew, David Hancock; and my uncle,
Terry Bailey—three men who left this world too soon.

gonefromthesewoods

chapterone

I didn't want to shoot a rabbit that cold November morning in 1992. Most men and boys I knew—and even some girls— lived to hunt wild game in the North Georgia woods that surrounded Newtonville.

But not me.

One day when I was five, I came up on Dad and his younger brother, Clay, skinning some rabbits they'd just killed in Sartain Woods. I tried not to breathe in the dead smell as Dad's big, rough hands ripped a rabbit's fur off like it was a candy bar wrapper. Right then, I decided hunting wasn't for me.

Uncle Clay had a different idea when he gave me Granddaddy Sartain's old .410 shotgun for my eleventh birthday. That gun, with its smooth walnut stock and long black barrel, had hung over the fireplace mantel in Clay's cabin for as long as I could remember.

"I didn't think I'd ever get Granddaddy's .410," I said, sighting down the barrel at a cardinal perched on a mimosa tree outside Clay's kitchen window. I hadn't ever thought about killing a bird, either. But I could feel the power of that possibility with Granddaddy's gun in my hands and my eye focused on those red feathers.

"Pop would have given you his shotgun before your eleventh birthday, if he was still around," Clay said. "It's past time you learned how to hunt and it don't look like your daddy is ever gonna stop drinking long enough to teach you."

I thought about Dad ripping that dead rabbit's skin off when I was five as I traced the swirl design on the gun's black metal faceplate with my finger. That firearm had felt good in my hands. Still, I couldn't imagine killing anything.

But if Clay said I ought to hunt, I figured I should at least give it a try. He got me started on reading comic books and now I couldn't put them down. So I slipped out of the house before daylight the next morning with my shotgun and followed Clay up Mouse Creek Road.

"Invited your daddy to come with us," Clay said in his deep voice as we walked in semidarkness along the ragged asphalt road edge.

"What'd he say?" I asked, trying to imagine Clay offering Dad that invitation. They were brothers, born from the same parents and raised together right here in Newtonville, in that cabin Clay still lived in. But Dad, who was thirteen years older, and Clay hardly ever spoke to each other unless they had to.

Mom said they hadn't gotten along since the car crash that killed their parents over on Hooper Gap Road when I was six. I can't remember much about that accident. I do know that Granddaddy's old green Ford pickup rammed into an oak tree. And that made Dad and Clay co-owners of the Sartain land—more than three hundred acres.

"Ray said he'd think about coming with us," Clay said. "Maybe he's still thinking about it right now in his warm bed. You ready to shoot some rabbit?"

"Past ready," I said, feeling the weight of the .410 in my gloved hands. "Bet I can get my limit today—all twelve."

I wasn't past ready to shoot anything, but that seemed like the right answer to Clay's question. What I really wanted to do was turn around. Turn around and sprint all the way home so I could crawl back into my own warm bed.

"You might have a better chance of bagging your limit if we got us some beagle dogs," Clay said, leaving the road and tramping across a meadow in his camouflage hunting boots.

I knew that some of the hunters around Newtonville used dogs, but I didn't think it mattered much if we had dogs or not. I was only hunting because Clay said I should try it. Who knew if I would ever hunt again?

Up ahead, I saw the sun, a glowing ball of light, spreading its yellow-orange color over the treetops. Maybe it'll warm up some, now that the sun's coming out, I thought, squaring my shoulders and crunching my boots against frosty grass, trying to walk like Clay as I followed him into the woods.

Our woods, Clay always said when he told me stories about our ancestors. The Sartains were some of the first settlers in Georgia. Hunting was how those pioneers survived, Clay said. No Winn-Dixies to feed them. They were on their own out here in the wilderness, with the Indians and the elements and wild animals.

I couldn't eat a piece of fried rabbit without thinking about Dad skinning that one when I was five. I was partial to grilled cheese sandwiches. The way Mom made them, oozing with marbled Colby-Jack. No one had to shoot those— or rip off their skin.

Clay glanced back over his shoulder at me as we headed up the pine-straw-covered path between the trees. "Better keep that shotgun pointed down, like I showed you last night," he said, snapping a branch with his heavy boots. "Can't be too careful when you're handling a firearm."

I looked at my gun, making sure it was pointed in the right direction. Clay had gone over safety rules in his cabin the night before. One of the things he'd told me was not to load the shotgun before I left the house this morning.

"Have it cocked open, ready for the shell," he'd said.

The round hole of the empty barrel stared back at me now like a black eye as I walked, shivering in my parka.

"When can I load?" I asked, feeling the sharp coldness chill my lungs as I inhaled pine-scented air, then let it whoosh out in a breath cloud.

"Wait till we get a little deeper into the woods," Clay answered. "You brought the cartridges, right?"

"Yep," I said, feeling to make sure the box with the rabbit picture on the side was in my coat pocket.

"Know what? Now that we're hunting partners, we really do need us a couple of dogs," Clay said, puffing his own warm breath clouds into the air. "They'd flush out every cottontail from here to town, huh, D-Man?"

To everyone else, my name was Daniel. But Clay, who had taught me everything I knew about superheroes, had nicknamed me D-Man one night about a year ago. We were playing touch football in the front yard, pretending we could see where we were going in the dim porch light with our secret X-ray vision.

"There goes Superman," Clay shouted when I dashed past him, winning the game. "Faster than a speeding bullet. More powerful than a locomotive—"

"Ah, you let me win, Clayton Eugene Sartain," I said, falling on the frosty grass, my heart pounding like it was going to explode beneath my Superman sweatshirt.

Clay sprawled beside me like a great big kid, even though he was twenty-two years old then. "Nope, you outran me, Daniel Russell Sartain. From now on, I'm calling you D-Man. That's your new secret superhero identity."

As usual, Mom was getting ready to go work the graveyard shift at the carpet mill later that night. Dad was in their bedroom, sleeping off some beers. He'd been a truck driver in the army before I was born. But for as long as I could remember, he hadn't worked a job. He'd pulled a government disability check out of the mailbox each month.

"Well?" Clay slowed down his long-legged walk and waited for me to catch up. "You never did answer my question. Don't you think we need us some dogs? Frank Hooper's favorite hunting dog just popped out a litter. What you say we adopt us a couple of pups?" He cut his eyes over at me to see if I was paying attention.

I knew Dad would never go for another dog at our house, especially if it was Clay's idea. So I said, "Dad pitched the biggest fit when Mom got Mitzi. I'm not even going to ask him if we can get another dog."

"Remember that hunting dog Ray had when you were little? Called him Lightning 'cause he ran so fast," Clay said. "Ray was crazy about that dog. You ought to ask him if you can get one of Hooper's puppies. He might say yes."

"I'll ask him tonight," I said, not wanting to ask Dad anything, but at the same time, thinking how great it would be to have a dog of my own. I wondered if I could make him more of a pet and less of a hunter.

"Good. I already told Old Man Hooper we'd take the beagles. We'll keep your dog at my place for a while," Clay said. "Go ahead and be picking out a name for yours. I'm calling mine Caesar. That's one tough dog name."

I grinned, wondering what I'd name my future dog, as we walked deeper into the woods. Maybe Dad would come around once he saw my pup.

"Too bad we don't have a dog right now," I said. And then an idea came to me. "Hey, I know. Maybe Mom would lend us Mitzi until the puppies are old enough to hunt. We could go back to the house and ask her. Bet she's up now, cooking cinnamon toast and scrambled cheese eggs."

"Mitzi?" Clay laughed so loud he upset a whole neighborhood of birds in the tree branches, making them twitter and squawk and flutter their wings. "You're joking, right? You don't really want us to go hunting with a prissy little Chihuahua dog, do you? What you think old Mitzi would do soon as she saw a rabbit?"

"Run like mad?" I snickered, imagining the scene. "Or

she'd go into one of her crazy shaking fits and pass out." Just like me, I thought, if I have to shoot the Easter bunny.

A damp, woodsy smell filled the air as we turned and headed up another path through the pines, dotted with occasional orange-and-gold-leaved hardwoods. A few more steps, and the trees parted. Sartain Lake spread out before us, all cool and misty. I could almost smell the fish, even though I knew it was too cold for them to be moving around much.

We stood there a minute, breathing in the damp lake air as mists moved slowly across the water. The trees around the lake were reflected in the cool surface, like they were looking at themselves in some giant's mirror.

Shivering, I watched a kingfisher dive down to the water. Canadian geese honked complaints when the blue-and-white feathered bird hovered for a moment, then hit the surface, plunging its beak into the rippling bluish green.

My stomach growled as the bird winged its way back over the treetops, a silvery bream wriggling in midair. We'd only been in the woods a few minutes and already my frozen-waffle energy was long gone.

I wonder how things would have turned out if I'd just done something different right then. Instead of standing there holding my gun, watching the kingfisher fly away with that fish. What if I'd thrown my .410 into the lake? If I try real hard, I can hear the splash. See the ripples circling round and round as the gun disappears, burying itself in the muddy lake bottom.

But that didn't happen.

"Go ahead and load," Clay said. "We're bound to run into a rabbit before long."

I took off my gloves and found the cartridge box in my coat pocket. Clay nodded his approval as I opened the top, removed one shell, and pushed it into the gun barrel.

A few minutes later, we came to the spot where our Sartain ancestors had built their first cabin more than a hundred years ago. Only thing left of that old place was the chimney. But I knew, from looking at gravestones in the family cemetery near Clay's cabin off Mouse Creek Road, that someone named Daniel had once lived here. I'd never seen a picture of him, but I bet he looked a lot like me.

As we walked on, deeper into the woods, I wondered how many rabbits that Daniel had shot. And if killing things had bothered him.

"Hey, D-Man, look at this," Clay said, squatting to examine something on the ground in front of him.

I was out of breath when I came up behind him and saw the rabbit—all flat on the pine straw with its legs extended, like it was still running. Its dark brown eyes were wide open, but I knew it couldn't see a thing.

"What happened?" I asked, panting. "I didn't hear any shots."

"Probably had a heart attack," Clay said. "Bet some predator chased him through the woods. Most likely a fox."

Clay peeled off one of his gloves. He reached down and touched the rabbit's grayish brown fur. Touched it real soft, like it might break if he wasn't careful.

"Hmm, still warm," Clay said. "I would bag him up and

take him home, but it's not much of a sport if you don't kill it yourself."

Clay got up. He took off his faded red cap and looked around the woods as if he half expected to see the predator watching us.

"Think I heard that fox just now," Clay said, putting his cap back on and looking at me. "You hear anything, D-Man?"

"Nothing but birds," I said, glancing away from the dead rabbit at a yellow-bellied sapsucker rat-a-tat-tatting its way up a tree trunk.

I hadn't even shot this rabbit, and it wasn't bleeding like the one Dad had skinned that time when I was five. Still, I couldn't look at it anymore. It made me wonder things. Like whether it hurt when it had the heart attack. And how come it had to die like that.

"Come on, let's get back to hunting," Clay said, following my gaze. "Supper's waiting for us out in these woods. All you gotta do is shoot it, huh, D-Man?"

"Gross," I groaned.

Clay gave me a sharp look. "What you mean, 'gross'? Fried rabbit is one of the top delicacies of the world. Can't you smell it already? And taste it? All warm and crispy and melt-in-your-mouth delicious? Life don't get much better than that."

"You know I'm not crazy about the taste of rabbit meat," I said. "And this dead rabbit . . . it looks a lot like the Easter bunny to me. Who wants to eat the Easter bunny unless it's made out of chocolate?"

"The Easter bunny?" Clay patted my shoulder like he felt

sorry for me. "Have you forgotten how old you are? You just had a birthday. You're eleven now—way too old to be thinking like that. Grow up."

I inhaled a deep breath of pine-scented air and let it out slowly as I looked at Clay, seeing the concern in his eyes. He wasn't making fun of my Easter bunny talk. He was worried about it. Worried that his nephew hadn't already given up little-kid stuff like that, even though Clay acted like a great big kid most of the time himself.

"Okay. You're right. Let's go shoot some rabbit." I tried to sound D-Man tough when I said those words. I didn't want Clay to think I was a baby.

"You'll get over those Easter bunny feelings when you shoot your first rabbit," Clay promised as we walked on through the cold woods, keeping our eyes alert for whatever was up ahead.

After a while, Clay stopped walking. He put his finger to his lips. "Shhh," he whispered, motioning at something in front of him. "Get ready, D-Man. This is your shot."

Sucking in my breath, I edged forward until I stood beside my uncle, tightening my hands on the .410. Up ahead, I spotted a small cottontail that could have been a twin of the dead rabbit. Frozen in place, it was trying to fool us into thinking it wasn't there at all.

"What you waiting for?" Clay whispered, moving closer to me. "Get into position. You know, like I showed you last night."

I dropped to one knee, feeling the chill of the ground through my jeans leg, and pushed the stock of my gun up against my right shoulder. The cold wood pressed my cheek. My .410 wobbled a little as I sighted along the barrel, using the tiny silver sight-post at the end to help me focus on the rabbit.

The hammer clicked as I cocked it back real slow with my thumb. Pricking up his ears, the rabbit sniffed the air but didn't run.

"You're ready," Clay whispered. "Don't be nervous. Control your breathing like I showed you and squeeze the trigger real easy."

I placed the tip of my finger against the trigger, squeezed slow, then stopped. How could I shoot this animal? I didn't even like the taste of rabbit meat. No way did I want to see this bunny bleed.

But I didn't want to disappoint Clay, either. He'd given me Granddaddy's shotgun, and he was set on me learning to hunt so I could kill things, like him and Dad and all the Sartain men before us. I had to pull the trigger, didn't I?

"That rabbit's got your name written all over it," Clay said, leaning closer until I could smell his sour coffee breath right above my head. "Shoot it. Quick. Before it takes off running."

I looked at the rabbit again, down the barrel of my gun. Closing my eyes, I saw Dad's big, rough hands ripping, ripping. Exposing pinkish gray skin with tiny globules of blood popping out all over.

When I didn't shoot, Clay's whisper-voice got louder. "You ever going to pull that trigger, D-Man? How you 'spect to hit a target with your eyes closed?"

"It's not a target," I whispered back, relaxing my finger again and opening my eyes. It was a living, breathing animal. With soft grayish brown fur and round bunny eyes.

"How long you think a wild animal like that lives anyway?" Clay said. "That rabbit's going to die whether you pull the trigger or not. You're a Sartain. Born hunter. That rabbit's game. Food for our table. Shoot it. That's what you're here for."

I looked back down my gun barrel at the frozen rabbit, flexing my finger against the trigger, trying to feel like a predator, a natural-born Sartain hunter. I could do this, couldn't I? All I had to do was squeeze . . . and *boom!* This rabbit would be history.

Lining the rabbit up again with the sight-post, I curled my finger against the trigger and started squeezing. Before I could pull the trigger all the way, the rabbit bolted up the path, disappearing in the tall underbrush between two pines.

"Guess that was the one that got away," Clay said, reaching down and patting my shoulder. "Don't worry about it. We'll find another rabbit in a minute. Might even run up on the same animal." Clay grinned at me, his face all red from the cold woods air.

I smiled back at my uncle. Smiled at him like I was happy that we'd find another rabbit to shoot. Maybe even the one that had run away just now. But really I was smiling because that rabbit wasn't dead. Because I hadn't shot my gun. Hadn't shot a hole in that grayish brown fur and made that little animal bleed all over the pine straw.

"Come on," Clay said. "You've got a lot more hunting to do."

I nodded and started getting up, letting the butt end of the shotgun press against the ground for support. My left hand still clutched the gun stock under the barrel, which slanted across my chest as I moved. I didn't think about my right-hand finger still on the trigger or how the cartridge was still loaded with the hammer cocked.

All I was thinking about was getting up. Getting up and following my uncle and being like him.

BOOM! A sound so loud my head felt like it might split open as I fell back to my knees. The gun seemed to fire all by itself, kicking against my arm like something alive.

Birds shrieked and scattered overhead as a small cloud of blue-gray smoke rose in the air beside me. I smelled gunpowder. And when I looked over, Clay slumped to his knees and fell forward, his face crashing into the pine straw.

chaptertwo

Have you ever felt like everything just stopped? Like the whole world froze and you were part of that ice? Unable to move. Barely breathing. Unsure of what to do next because you'd never been to a place like that before?

That's how I felt, kneeling out there in the woods by my uncle. The boom of the shotgun blast still rang in my ears. I felt myself go all white and ghostly like the comic book character Deadman as I looked at Clay. Facedown on the pine straw. Blond hair curling on the back of his neck. Wrinkled camouflage jacket. The muddy heels of his boots. And in front of him, his hat, upside down where it had landed when he fell.

This wasn't real.

I waited for Clay to move, to say something. When he didn't, I swallowed and forced my voice, hoarse and shaky, up my throat.

"Clay?"

No answer.

I leaned over and grabbed his arm and shook it gently, not wanting to believe how limp it felt.

"Clay?" My voice squeaked into the woods air, thin as a scared bird's cry.

Nothing.

I hugged myself, trembling, wondering what to do. This was an emergency and I had to act fast. But I'd never had a lifesaving course, so I didn't know how to do CPR. Any other time, I would have asked Clay what to do. But today, in the woods, I'd have to figure everything out myself.

Just thinking about how far we were from my house made me shake harder. We were at least two miles from Mouse Creek Road. "Stop thinking about that," I told myself, forcing my eyes to look back down at Clay.

Was he breathing? I couldn't tell. I'd have to turn him over. I pushed at his back, then stopped. My teeth chattered as I tried to calm myself. I wanted to help my uncle, but I was afraid to turn him over. He might be bleeding.

But he wasn't dead. He couldn't be dead. No way.

I got up, shivering, wondering what to do. I couldn't turn Clay over and I couldn't keep looking at his back, so still and scary. The loud, rasping scream of a red-tailed hawk made me turn my eyes toward the trees. The bird circled in the sky between two pines.

I wanted the hawk to dive down into Sartain Woods and snatch me out of this frozen place. Jab my arm with its sharp beak. Lift me up by the shoulder of my parka and fly me away from what had just happened to Clay.

I was thinking that, imagining it, when my heart came back to life, pounding hard inside my chest like it wanted to escape. The front of my jeans felt suddenly wet and cold as I turned back to Clay and dropped to my knees, leaning over him, trembling, feeling like I might pass out.

Grabbing his shoulder, I nudged him over on his back.

I gasped when I saw Clay's eyes. Open with the same far-away look I'd seen on that first rabbit earlier this morning. Only blue instead of brown. Deep Sartain blue . . . glinting from streaks of sunlight shining through the treetops overhead, but not seeing.

Maybe Clay was sleeping. You could sleep with your eyes open, couldn't you? I'd seen Dad do it a few times in his recliner after supper.

"Please wake up, Clay," I begged. His skin had turned a pale gray color, like the underbelly of a fish. The green and tan camouflage material of his hunting jacket couldn't hide the circle of blood spreading across the front.

"You can't be dead." I got up, trying to choke back something in my throat. Maybe he was unconscious. I'd watched a lot of *Doogie Howser, M.D.* TV shows with Mom. People got hurt all the time on TV. Dr. Doogie knew how to put them back together. Clay needed a doctor right now. I had to get him to the hospital in Newtonville—fast.

"Help, *help!*" I screamed. I yelled for help again, over and over, until my voice sounded hoarse and broken. Then I stopped yelling. No one could hear me. We were deep in Sartain Woods, in the middle of our three hundred acres. There weren't any roads through this part of our land. All we had was the path, and it was barely wide enough for two people to walk on.

I looked at Clay again, at his gray-skinned, bloody-coat stillness. Then I stumbled over to some bushes and vomited up my breakfast. Waffle, syrup, butter all came gurgling out, tasting as horrible as I felt.

Still heaving, I wiped my tongue on my coat sleeve, gagging at the stench, trying to blot out that sick taste.

I stumbled back to Clay's side. Only thing that had changed was the circle of blood growing bigger and bigger. I didn't want to leave my uncle bleeding out there in the woods, but I had to go for help.

Clay had shown me a shortcut to Mouse Creek Road once, off the path and through the trees. I got up and started running, trying not to look back at Clay on the ground, but looking anyway until I was too far away.

Low-hanging branches scratched my face as I ran, weaving my way through the pines, stumbling, scrambling back to my feet, running hard as I could, on and on through the woods until I got to Mouse Creek.

The cold, gurgling water seeped into my boots, wetting my pant legs as I splashed my way across, trying to keep my balance in the rippling currents. I struggled up the muddy creek bank, slipping back into the red mud slime a couple of times, then ran full-speed, wondering if I'd ever find the road.

A few minutes later, I burst out of the woods and stumbled onto the edge of Mouse Creek Road. Doubling over, I coughed and dry-heaved. Then, making myself stand, I scanned the road, shaking and straining to hear any car sounds coming my way.

For a long time, nobody came. I was alone on the asphalt. All I could see of town in the distance was the tin-roofed steeple of Newtonville Methodist Church. Looking the other way, I saw our house, a tiny white speck surrounded by trees. How long would it take me to get there?

My wet boots made slapping sounds on the pavement as I took off running toward home. Pumping my legs, pushing myself harder, feeling the air heave in and out of my tired lungs. Clay would be okay if I got help. Doctors could do miracles.

Up ahead, I spotted our neighbor Frank Hooper's dented, dirty-white Ford pickup coming toward me.

"Stop!" I screamed, waving my arms.

Brakes screeched as Mr. Hooper slowed the old truck and eased it to the side of the road. The old man got out, and dogs barked and howled inside the camper-top-covered truck bed.

"What's wrong, boy?" Mr. Hooper looked me over, sizing me up with milky eyes blinking through the thick lenses of old-fashioned horn-rimmed glasses.

"My uncle," I blurted, trying to slow down my breathing as I hurried over to the truck. "He's been shot."

"Clay? That's terrible, boy. Where is he?" Mr. Hooper looked past me, like he expected to see Clay.

"In the woods," I said, pointing toward the spot I'd come from, back up the road. I tried to keep from shaking as I looked at Mr. Hooper. "Past the lake. Clay's hurt bad. We've got to get help."

I thought Mr. Hooper would ask a lot of questions, but he didn't. He said, "Hunting accident?"

I nodded.

The old man got back in his truck, breathing hard as he reached across the cracked vinyl seat and grabbed a brick-sized gadget that looked like a cross between a phone and a portable radio. He pressed it against his ear, cleared his throat, then barked out, "K3NPA CQ," in a rusty voice.

"Sheriff's deputy is on his way—and the paramedics," Hooper said when he'd finished talking. "They're dispatching the game warden, too, since it's a hunting accident."

I nodded, wondering how Mr. Hooper had said all that into the radio phone using only a few real words.

"Bet you didn't know I was a ham," Hooper said, helping me into the truck. I wrinkled my nose at the smell of dogs. The beagles in back barked and jumped, crashing their heads against the truck's window.

"A ham?" I asked, grabbing on to the armrest on the door as Hooper cranked the truck.

"Ham radio operator. I always carry my handheld in the truck. Never know when it might come in handy. Show me where you came out of the woods." Mr. Hooper looked past me through the side window as he drove. "Help will be here any minute. But you've got to lead us to the scene, boy."

I nodded, feeling my teeth chatter as the dogs continued to bark and moan in back.

Hooper looked at me. "Calm down. Those paramedics will know what to do for your uncle. Hunting accidents happen all the time, and hunters sometimes shoot things they weren't hunting for. You know that, boy."

"Yeah," I said in a weak voice, turning my face to the window, watching trees go by in a pine-needled blur.

But accidents like this aren't supposed to happen to my uncle, I thought. How could somebody over six feet tall get cut down like a pine tree in the woods? Clay was tough. He'd probably be up and wiping himself off when we got there.

"Here!" I shouted, almost bumping my face against the window glass. "Pull over. This is where I came out. It's a shortcut to the deep woods."

Mr. Hooper stomped the brake pedal, making the truck tires skid against the asphalt. He shifted gears and eased the truck to the side of the road. I opened the door and almost fell as I slipped off the seat to the ground. Was this really the place? I wasn't sure as I took off running toward the trees.

"Wait a minute, boy!" Mr. Hooper shouted after me.

Just as I darted into the woods, he grabbed my arm and pulled me back, spinning me around.

"Give the ambulance and the authorities a minute or two to get here. They won't know where to go if you're not here to show 'em." Mr. Hooper's milky eyes squinted at me through the thick lenses of his glasses.

I nodded, feeling my breathing slow down as I walked back to the truck with Mr. Hooper.

After that, everything blurred together. The shrill sound of sirens making me cover my ears as emergency vehicles raced toward us from town.

Red and blue lights flashing everywhere.

Me leading a parade of paramedics, sheriff's deputies,

the game warden, and Mr. Hooper on a long hike through the trees.

All of us splashing through Mouse Creek, then sprinting fast as we could to the place where Clay lay bleeding.

One look at Clay with all that blood spreading across his hunting jacket made me fall on the ground, bawling, beating the pine straw with my fists, wishing I'd never come out here in the woods with that gun.

The game warden, one of the tallest men I'd ever seen, came over and dropped to the ground beside me, pressing his big face against the pine straw, looking right into my eyes.

I turned my face away and watched a sheriff's deputy stretch yellow crime-scene tape from tree to tree. The dispenser made sharp tearing sounds each time the deputy pulled tape off the roll. And I felt each rip somewhere deep inside.

"You doing all right, son?" the game warden asked.

I shook my head and stared at the yellow tape, wishing I could make it all disappear.

"I know you don't feel like talking, but it's my job to ask you what happened out here this morning. You understand?"

"No!" The word shot out of me before I could stop it. I don't understand anything, I thought, grinding my cheek into the prickly pine straw, making my skin hurt as I lay there, wishing the game warden would go away.

I didn't understand, but somehow I answered his questions, forcing each hard word up my throat and spitting it out at the game warden like it was a bone I'd swallowed and was choking on.

When he'd finished questioning me, the game warden got up and brushed the dirt and straw off his tan uniform. I felt how strong he was as he pulled me up, too. When he walked us toward Mr. Hooper, I tried not to look at the ground where Clay was. But my eyes slid over there anyway.

Clay was gone. In his place, someone had put a small blue plastic marker. Near that, the ground was all wet with blood. The game warden turned my face the other way with his hand as we walked by the accident site. But he couldn't stop the air from reeking with that dead smell.

"Could you take this boy home, Frank?" the game warden asked when we got to the other side of the site, where Mr. Hooper stood, picking bark off a pine tree.

"Sure thing, Nick." Mr. Hooper gathered me up in his arms, carrying me through the woods like I was one of his beagle dogs and I'd hurt myself. I buried my face in the scratchy wool of his doggy-smelling coat as the old man took me to his truck and tucked me inside.

"That yellow tape had the words 'Crime Scene Do Not Cross' all over it," I said.

"I know," Mr. Hooper said, starting the motor, then turning the truck toward our house. "Game warden said that's what they have to do till they rule it an accident. He's just following procedure. Nobody thinks you shot your uncle on purpose, boy. Accidents happen. And then we have to deal with them."

When we got to my house, Mr. Hooper honked the horn. He slipped out of the truck and helped me down from the seat like I was crippled and couldn't walk by myself anymore.

Dad burst out of our house then, and Mom followed, wiping her hands on a red checked dish towel.

"What is it, Daniel . . . what happened?" Mom put her hands on my face. She looked me up and down, her brown eyes searching for clues.

Dad glanced at me with a puzzled look on his way to Mr. Hooper's truck. The two men stood there, talking in low voices. I heard Clay's name a couple of times—and mine.

Finally, Dad turned and looked at me. His lips made a mean, straight line on his face as he glared with cold eyes.

"There's been an accident," Dad said, turning toward Mom. "Clay's at the hospital. Frank's taking me over there. Give you a call when I know something."

The vinyl seat squeaked as Dad climbed into the passenger side of Mr. Hooper's truck and slammed the door. Dad rolled down the window and pointed his finger at me. "Daniel, get on some clean clothes. You stink like pee."

chapterthree

After four tries, Mr. Hooper's truck sputtered to life. The two men moved like a pair of bobble-head dolls in the old pickup's cab as Mom and I watched the truck go down our long, rutted driveway.

"Old Man Hooper needs to step on it—he's going so slow," I said.

Mom curled her arm around my shoulder and pulled me into her side. She leaned down and snuggled her nose into my hair, breathing me in and hugging my body hard like she didn't ever want to let go.

"I figured you'd get home soon. But you surprised me, showing up with Frank Hooper," Mom said, her mountain-twangy words puffing my hair as she talked. "Hope Clay's not hurt too bad."

I buried my face in Mom's soft Seekers Sunday School

Class T-shirt, breathing in the familiar dusty smell of talcum powder mixed with cinnamon from her breakfast toast.

"Thank goodness you're all right," Mom said, hugging me harder. "Don't know what I'd do if anything happened to you, Daniel."

Mom came from Soddy-Daisy, Tennessee, a little town about fifteen miles from Chattanooga. She'd met up with Dad when he took a fishing trip to Tennessee one summer with Clay and Granddaddy Sartain. They stayed at a state park not far from Soddy-Daisy and ate in this little restaurant called JJ's Bar-B-Cue, where Mom worked.

Dad was different back then, Mom said. "Full of fun and raring to go" was how she put it in her mountain talk.

Sometimes Mom told me stories about her growing-up days in Soddy-Daisy. About the rivers and mountains and the neat old farmhouse with the wraparound porch. I wanted to go there and see everything for myself. Breathe in the sweet mountain air. Swim in the Soddy River. But Dad didn't get along with Mom's family, so he'd never let me make the trip.

"What happened to Clay?" Mom asked, turning me toward the porch and walking me up the concrete steps into the house. "Did some hunter mistake him for a rabbit? Bet y'all went past the lake, into the deep woods."

"He got shot," I said in a quiet voice.

"Clay's shot? Is he okay, Daniel? How bad is he hurt?"

Mom's expression of shock made me turn away. I couldn't look at her right now. If I did, I might start crying. So I let my eyes wander across our living room and kitchen, all one big room with just a half-wall separating it.

"Daniel? You listening to me?" Mom's voice sounded scared now. "What happened to Clay?"

I made myself look at Mom. What was I going to tell her? Why couldn't she stop asking me questions? Clay was going to be okay.

He was at the hospital right now. And they were fixing him like they fixed everybody on TV. So he could come back and play football and Nintendo and read comics.

We hadn't even finished "The Mystery of the Mild-Mannered Superman." And tonight we were going to watch a *Circus of the Stars* show Clay had taped on his VCR. He wouldn't miss that show for anything.

"We ought to join the circus," Clay had said one night last week, clasping his hands together and trying to loop his arms all the way over his head without letting go, like a trapeze artist on the circus show.

"Speak for yourself, weirdo," I teased, punching Clay's muscled arm, making him mess up his trick big-time.

"Circus folks ain't weird," Clay said. "They're just different. Forget the arm stunts. How much fun could we have, all covered in scales like Reptile Man?"

"No way would I be a snake," I told him.

But I felt like a snake now, covered with scales as I stared back at Mom with shifty yellow reptile eyes. I couldn't help thinking that if I opened my mouth, a forked snake tongue might dart out as I told her what I'd done to Clay.

"Tell me what happened, Daniel. You know you can tell me anything, no matter what." Mom had a nervous catch in her voice now, like she was afraid to hear what I might say next.

I was afraid to hear my own scared voice tell Mom what I'd done. She thought somebody else had shot Clay this morning—not her own son. What was she going to think when I told her the shooter was me?

But I had to tell her. So I took a deep breath and forced the words out. "*I shot him.*"

"*What?*"

Horror flashed in Mom's eyes, and it made me feel awful—like I'd shot her, too. Like I'd taken Granddaddy's .410 and fired a cartridge right into my mom. I could see the pain of what I'd done to Clay hurting her, making her face morph into lines and creases that gave her the look of being a lot older than her twenty-nine years.

I wanted to run away then—go hide in my room and never come out. But my muscles and joints were frozen.

Mom's mouth opened and closed, then opened again. She pressed her pale hand against her forehead and the words "Oh my Lord" came out into the room between us.

We both jumped as Mitzi's tiny toenails skittered across the kitchen tiles and into the living room. Stopping by the fireplace, panting, the dog stared up at me with her brown rat face, trembling like she knew what had happened to Clay.

"Daniel, you wouldn't shoot your uncle. You love Clay."

"I shot him, Mom. I didn't mean to shoot him, Mom, I . . ."

My voice stopped working then. It felt like all the energy that powered my vocal cords a few seconds earlier had switched inside me and started pumping water to my tear ducts.

I knew crying was a baby thing, a silly, stupid thing that eleven-year-old boys like me were never supposed to do. But I didn't feel like an eleven-year-old boy anymore. I watched Mitzi shake by the fireplace. Then I turned to Mom and she looked at me with a pained expression, like she was trying to decide whether to keep on loving me or to hate me forever for what I'd done to Clay. And I let those tears go, feeling the salty wetness slide down my face.

Mom got a clean dish towel from the kitchen. She wiped my tears away like I was a little toddler, making the skin on my face tingle from the rough terry cloth.

"No," she said softly, pressing water out of the corners of my eyes. "You wouldn't shoot anybody on purpose, Daniel. I know that."

Mom leaned into me and kissed the tip of my nose, her cinnamon breath warm against my skin.

"You surprised me, going hunting with Clay this morning. I know how you are, Daniel. You've got the Sartain name. But you're more like a Russell—like my daddy back in Soddy-Daisy.

"When he was a boy, his mama used to pack him a bag of cheese biscuits and a jar of iced tea and let him slip out of the house and sleep in the woods at hog-killin' time. He never had no use for slaughtering things. Even if they tasted delicious all battered and fried up in an iron skillet."

Mom sucked in her breath real quick and I saw her pink lips tremble the way they always did when she was nervous about something.

"Is Clay okay, Daniel? Where'd you shoot him? In the leg? The shoulder? Where?" Mom had tears in her eyes now.

Dark little mascara rivers trickled down her cheeks as she waited for my answer.

The color red flashed in my mind. Damp, dark red spreading across Clay's jacket. "His chest. The pellets from the cartridge went in his chest." I spat the foul-tasting words out, looking away from Mom at the blank TV screen. It was still Saturday morning. I ought to be watching cartoons.

I wanted to flip on the TV and watch Bugs Bunny. Clay's favorite Bugs cartoon was "Rabbit Fire." Elmer Fudd hunting Bugs Bunny and Daffy Duck.

"Is it rabbit season or duck season?" Clay liked to ask, making his voice sound all sputtery like Fudd's.

Whatever was left in my stomach churned and threatened to bubble up my throat as I thought about Clay watching that cartoon with me. I probably wouldn't ever watch a cartoon again—unless Clay could watch with me. He'd be doing that again, wouldn't he?

"Oh, my goodness." Mom slumped back on our orange-and-brown-flowered sofa and buried her face in her hands, shaking her head. "Clay's not okay, is he, Daniel?"

I put my arms around Mom and clung to her while she sobbed. Mitzi trotted over to us, shaking and moaning her scared dog sounds.

"Is he dead, Daniel?" Mom asked. She wiped at her eyes, smudging the mascara into a wet, black mess on her cheeks.

"No," I answered real quick, like that would make the word true. Clay couldn't be dead. He was strong like Spider-Man and Superman and all the other superheroes we read about in comics. Those paramedics had worked on him in the ambulance, and the emergency room doctors were making him good as new. He probably wasn't even bleeding anymore.

The phone rang, a shrill sound that made us both jump. Mom got up and stumbled into the kitchen. Grabbing the tan receiver from the wall, she dropped it, then caught it as it dangled by the cord, and pressed it to her ear. Her tear-stained face got wetter as she listened and talked into the receiver in a hushed voice.

Mom hung up the phone, slapping it hard on its cradle. She bowed her head. I saw her lips tremble, then move in a silent prayer. When she finished praying, her eyes blinked open and she looked at me and said, "That was your dad calling from the hospital."

chapterfour

Mom walked back to the sofa and sat beside me, cupping her warm hand over mine. She looked right into me and I could see my own scared face reflected in her eyes.

"Clay's gone, Daniel," Mom said, her voice quivering. "One of the pellets from the shotgun cartridge pierced his heart—"

"*No!*" I pulled my hand away from Mom and pounded it on the sofa cushion. "Clay's not dead. No way. They're fixing him at the hospital. Operating. Giving him oxygen. Just like they do on TV. Dad and Mr. Hooper are bringing him back home right now."

Mom grabbed my hand. "No, Daniel. Clay probably died right after the accident . . . out there in the woods." Mom squeezed my hand and tried to pull me close for a hug, but I didn't move. This couldn't be happening. Clay was coming back. He had to come back.

"They said Clay didn't feel a thing," Mom told me in be-tween sobs.

Didn't feel a thing? How could a shotgun pellet pierce your heart without you feeling a thing? For a moment, I saw that first rabbit in the woods—the one that had been run-ning before its heart suddenly stopped. Did that rabbit feel a thing? Did Clay?

But Mom had said he was dead and that made it true. This wasn't fair. Why did my uncle have to die like that? Out there in the woods like a rabbit?

The answer came to me in a searing blast of pain. Clay had died because of me. *Me*. Daniel Russell Sartain. His stu-pid nephew who couldn't pull the trigger—until the wrong time. Couldn't take his shot with the rabbit right there, standing still and ready. Couldn't shoot a rabbit. Even girls could shoot a rabbit.

But not me. Clay was dead because of me. I was an uncle killer. And I didn't know how I was going to live with that.

Mom brushed hair out of my eyes with her fingers. She looked at me for a long time, taking in my vomit-stained sleeve and my pee-soaked jeans. "I'd better call Dr. Harris," she said. "But let's find you some clean clothes first."

• • •

Mom fixed me a grilled cheese sandwich and some tomato soup for lunch. The sandwich didn't even taste like food as I tried to chew it. And one look at the steaming mug of soup and I was right back there in the woods with all that blood.

Our family doctor came by that afternoon, wearing a red Atlanta Falcons sweatshirt instead of his white doctor's coat. He gave me an exam right there in our living room—to make sure I didn't have any physical injuries from the accident, he said.

Dr. Harris called in a prescription, and the Newtonville pharmacy delivered the amber-colored container of pills within the hour. I didn't want to take the medicine, but Mom insisted, saying it would help me sleep.

I slept that afternoon and night and all through Sunday, getting up every now and then and stumbling down the hall to the bathroom. When I woke up late Monday morning, Mom was sitting by me on my bed.

"You needed that rest, Daniel," she said, smoothing the hair on my forehead. "Now it's time for you to get up. I could use some company," she added, helping me out of bed and walking me to the bathroom.

My face in the medicine cabinet mirror over the sink looked scary. Blond hair stuck out all over my head, like some wild comic book villain's. I traced the big, dark circles under my eyes.

Back in my room, instead of putting on my clothes, like Mom wanted me to, I climbed into bed and pulled the warm quilt up over my villain hair. Why should I stay up? I didn't even feel like me anymore. I just wanted to sink down into the warmth of my bed and disappear.

"Daniel?" Mom called from the kitchen.

When I didn't answer, she came into my room and pulled the covers away from my face and maneuvered me into a sitting position. "Maybe this will give you the strength to get up," she said, holding out a bowl of oatmeal.

She handed me a spoon, then pulled my desk chair over by the bed and sat there, waiting for me to dig in.

I watched tiny wisps of oatmeal-scented steam swirl into the air. Then, staring down into the bowl of melting butter and brown sugar mush, I heard my stomach growl. It didn't matter if my stomach was empty. I didn't deserve to eat.

"You need to eat," Mom said, leaning over and taking the spoon out of my hand. "You slept for over twenty-four hours. You must be hungry."

"Not really," I said as she brought a spoonful of oatmeal up to my lips and pressed the food into my mouth like I was a baby.

I wanted to spit out the gooey mush, but Mom insisted that I eat a few bites.

"Good boy," she said, patting my wild hair down with her fingers. She got up and gave me a light kiss on my forehead. "I'll get you some milk. You'll feel better before you know it."

Mom was right. A little while later, I felt strong enough to camp out on the living room sofa with Mitzi curled against my legs for most of the morning and afternoon.

Our phone rang constantly as the hunting-accident story spread through Newtonville.

"Why can't Dad get the phone for once?" I asked,

pulling the dog into my lap and scratching the fur on her neck.

"He's out taking care of some business," Mom said as she dashed into the kitchen to answer another call.

Mitzi pricked up her ears and moaned at the sounds of footsteps on our porch. I thought there'd be a knock. Instead we heard the clunk of something being placed on the table by the door.

"The neighbors are trying to comfort us," Mom said as she brought in another tinfoil-covered dish. "But Lord-a-mercy, I don't know what we're going to do with all this food."

I didn't feel comforted, and after that oatmeal, I wasn't hungry. I just wanted to forget about what had happened to Clay out in the woods. Maybe if I could blot it out of my mind, it hadn't really happened.

I got up and walked over to the window and looked out across our porch, down the long driveway to Mouse Creek Road. Had it only been two days since Clay and I had walked there?

Don't think about that, I told myself, turning my eyes away, squeezing them shut to hold back the wetness.

"That was Mrs. Pettibone," Mom said, hanging up the phone. "Your teacher's coming by with the school counselor."

"*Now?*" I groaned.

"After school lets out—in about forty-five minutes," Mom said.

I'd hardly had time to slip on a clean pair of jeans and

a fresh flannel shirt before the two women showed up at our door.

"The game warden, Nick Fortson, called and told me about the accident," Mrs. Pettibone said, towering over Mom in her black and white checked pantsuit as they shook hands. "Nick was one of my students years ago."

Mom nodded, looking past my teacher at the tiny woman walking in behind her.

"I'd like you to meet our school counselor, Lisa Hardy," Mrs. Pettibone added, gesturing toward the red-haired woman in a rumpled denim jacket.

"I hope it's okay for us to talk to Daniel now," Mrs. Hardy said in a cheerful voice, making me sit up straight on the couch with her sharp, intelligent look.

"We won't stay long, I promise," Mrs. Pettibone said. "We just want to touch base with you and offer some help." My teacher gave Mom her most dazzling smile, the one she reserved for students who never came in tardy.

Mom smiled back, though I could see it took a lot of effort for her to make her lips curl up at the corners.

I knew exactly how she felt as I watched Mrs. Pettibone and Mrs. Hardy arrange themselves in two folding chairs near the sofa. My teacher held a big white envelope in her lap. The counselor clutched a briefcase and stared at a fist-sized crack in the green plaster wall, near our redbrick fireplace.

There's something unnatural about seeing your teacher and the school counselor sitting in your living room. Looking around at your family pictures. Staring at ashtrays full of Dad's stinky cigarette butts. Talking to your mom.

Mom sank into her big oak rocker with the cane-bottomed seat. It was one of the few things she'd brought with her from Soddy-Daisy after she married Dad.

Mrs. Pettibone had her mouth open to say something. Mrs. Hardy was smiling at me, with a look in her eyes like she knew what my teacher was going to say. And Mom was rocking pretty hard when we heard motor noises in the driveway. The sounds of heavy footsteps on the porch made us all look at the door.

I was expecting the sound of another casserole dish on the porch table. Instead, the door opened with a loud cracking noise and Dad walked in, his beard-stubbled face all flushed from the cold air outside.

Dad looked at my teacher and the counselor like they were selling something he didn't want.

"This is my husband, Ray," Mom said in a nervous voice.

"Nice to finally meet you, Mr. Sartain," Mrs. Pettibone said. She smiled at Dad, but her smile wasn't dazzling. "I'm so sorry about what happened. And I'm sorry I haven't met you before at Daniel's parent-teacher conferences. You have a fine son, you know."

"Yes, we were hoping the whole family would be here," Mrs. Hardy said, looking Dad over with her inquiring eyes.

Dad's lips turned inward, folding into a mean, straight line. He huffed out a breath, then said, "Well, it's a shame the *whole* family ain't here."

"You're right." Mrs. Hardy glanced at Mrs. Pettibone, exchanging some secret counselor look with my teacher.

Dad didn't stick around for any more teacher or counselor

talk. He looked at the refrigerator and I knew he was think-ing about getting a beer.

But he didn't go into the kitchen. He tromped down the hall into the bedroom and slammed the door.

Mom looked embarrassed. Both of our visitors looked like they were making notes in their head.

"This is for you, Daniel," Mrs. Pettibone said, getting up and handing me the envelope she'd brought. "All your class-mates signed the card. We're so sorry about what happened."

What kind of card do you give someone who shot his uncle? I wondered, putting the envelope on the coffee table, on top of a stack of Mom's magazines. Whatever the card said, I couldn't look right now.

I heard bumping noises in the bedroom. What was Dad doing in there? Was he coming back in here or what?

The counselor took Mom aside in the kitchen while Mrs. Pettibone talked to me about being strong and getting plenty of rest and coming back to school as soon as I felt up to it.

I listened to my teacher, but at the same time I listened for Dad. I watched Mom and Mrs. Hardy in the kitchen, too, and tried to hear what they were saying. They kept their voices low—Mom's mountain twang and Mrs. Hardy's singsong, perfect English blending together like a weird grown-up harmony.

Several times I heard my name. And Mom trying to ex-plain Dad's behavior. Mrs. Hardy said something about a counselor. Mom nodded and looked toward the bedroom.

As the women left, I stood at the window and watched the tan Toyota bump down the driveway. The car was a tiny dot moving up Mouse Creek Road like a Matchbox toy when I heard Dad burst out of his bedroom.

I didn't want to turn around, but I did. Dad's lips were folded into that mean line.

The hair at the back of my neck bristled as I waited for Dad to speak. My dad was mostly a lot of ugly words, especially when he'd been drinking. But every now and then, he exploded for real.

Like one time when I was eight and Dad pulled off his black leather belt. He striped my legs so bad I could hardly walk that day—just because I hadn't taken out the trash before he got home.

I glanced away from Dad at the trash can in the kitchen by the refrigerator. Was it full? I couldn't tell.

"What was that all about? Those women had no business coming here," Dad said. Turning his eyes toward Mom, he gritted his teeth, shaking with rage.

"Calm down, Ray. They're just trying to help," Mom said. She walked over to Dad and tried to take his arm.

He jerked it back and held it in the air with his fist balled like a warning.

"Get away from me, Melissa!" he shouted.

"Okay," Mom answered. She came over to me then and stood there with her arm around my shoulder, like it was two against one.

Dad stared back at Mom and, for a minute, I thought he might use his fist on her, even though I'd never seen him do that before. Then his expression changed from mean to sad.

"Oh, oh, *oh*," Dad moaned, holding his head and shaking

violently. "I can't take this. This is not . . . this is too much like when Mama and Daddy died . . . this is . . . *Oh!*"

I was really scared then and I saw fright in Mom's face, too. I'd never seen Dad this bad before. And I was afraid to see what might come next.

chapterfive

"What you looking at, Daniel?"

Dad wasn't holding his head anymore. His eyes burned into me like a pair of his stinky cigarettes. Cupping one big, rough hand inside the other, he cracked his knuckles, taking his time, making each finger joint pop like he was getting his fist ready for action.

Mom pulled me closer until I felt her heart beating a nervous rhythm against my forehead.

"I asked you a question, son. If you're such a fine young man, like your teacher said, how come you can't answer?"

Dad got wild then. He kicked at our sofa. He grabbed one of Mom's ginger-jar lamps and shook it, then set it down hard on the lamp table, making Mitzi scurry into the kitchen, whining and looking back at Dad with bulging dog eyes.

"Ray," Mom pleaded. "Get ahold of yourself. We're all heartsick and upset."

The phone rang, shrill and loud. Mom moved toward the kitchen to answer. The sound of footsteps on our porch made her turn back toward the front door. We heard muffled voices, then the clunk of something—probably another casserole—being left there to comfort us.

Dad pressed his hands over his ears and closed his eyes, screwing them up tight like he was trying to shut everything out.

"Ray, why don't you go back in the bedroom and lie down," Mom suggested.

Dad opened his eyes wide, shook his head, then looked around the living room, at the pictures on the wall, the sofa, Mom's oak rocker.

Mom liked to tell how she had rocked me through long nights of colic when I was a baby in that old chair.

Dad walked over and grabbed the rocker by its arms. He heaved it up over his head like it was made of paper instead of golden oak.

"No, Ray!" Mom screamed.

Dad ignored Mom. He stood there, balancing the heavy chair high in the air, his arms trembling. His face was all puckered and red, and the line of his mouth looked so tense and tight I thought it might slice his face in two.

"Put my chair down, Ray," Mom demanded. "*Now!* You're not the only one grieving over what happened to Clay." Mom moved closer as she talked, letting her nervous eyes dart from Dad's face to the rocker and back again.

Dad lowered the chair a little at a time until it was close

enough to the floor to let it drop. It made a loud cracking noise, but I didn't see any broken places.

"Humph," Dad said, looking satisfied, like he'd done something good instead of almost destroying Mom's favorite piece of furniture.

Mom stared hard at Dad, looking like she might bust out crying. Instead, she walked over to her chair and eased back into it, testing it to make sure it wasn't going to fall apart.

I listened to the squeak-squawk as Mom rocked, patting the chair arms with her hands. I wanted to go sit with her, like I used to when I was little. But I couldn't move.

Dad walked to the kitchen and pulled a beer out of the refrigerator. He popped the top and took a long, slow drink, his Adam's apple bobbing.

"What's this?" Dad asked, grabbing a piece of paper from the countertop. He moved his mouth, saying the words to himself as he read. "Counseling? No." He crumpled the paper and tossed it at the trash can.

"Ray, we've got to talk," Mom said, rocking harder.

Dad took another swig of beer and looked at Mom like he was trying to decide if talking was what he wanted to do right then. While he was deciding, I slipped down the hall to my room and locked the door behind me.

● ● ●

I woke up later that night screaming. The nightmare seemed so real, I thought if only I yelled at Clay loud enough, he would open his eyes and get up from that bloody pine straw.

Pulling the quilt over my face, barely breathing through the old cotton cloth, I thought about how my uncle wasn't ever going to wake up. The more I thought about that, the madder I felt. Why did this happen to Clay? And me. Why did it happen to me?

"Daniel, you okay in there?" Mom's soft voice in the hallway. I heard my doorknob rattle as she tried to come in. The lock kept her out.

She tapped on the door. "I won't be going in to work tonight. Boss called and gave me a week off from the plant. Listen, your daddy just got all wound up today. He didn't break my chair, you know. He put it down. Everything is okay now. He was just upset."

Mom waited a minute, giving me time to say something. But I was busy thinking about what she'd said.

Her chair didn't get broken. But Clay got broken out there in the woods. I got broken, too. I'd been too numb to feel anything at first. Now I felt jagged edges all over. They hurt. Hurt like my whole body was nothing but broken bones jabbing through tender skin.

Mom was trying to comfort me. She understood how hard it was after what happened. But Dad was acting worse than ever.

"You missed supper, hon. You must be starving," Mom said through the door. "One of the neighbors brought your favorite—chicken and dumplings. I'll fix you a bowl."

"I'm not hungry, Mom." I didn't have a favorite food anymore. Or a favorite anything.

The phone rang in the kitchen.

"Be right back," Mom said.

I should unlock my door, I thought. And eat. Maybe that would make this terrible feeling in the pit of my stomach go away. Taking a deep breath, I raised my head, then flopped it back on the pillow, too exhausted to move.

In a minute, Mom was back in the hall, rattling my doorknob. "Daniel? Can't you unlock this door? You doing okay in there?"

How could I be doing okay? My body hurt all over and my mind kept going back to that nightmare in the woods. I curled into a ball under my covers, hugging myself tight.

"That was the game warden. He's waiting for the state crime lab autopsy results. And they're doing some tests on your gun."

I heard Mom sniffling in the hall, but still I couldn't make myself talk to her. I was like a roly-poly bug now, all rolled up and closed to the world. No matter what Mom said or did or offered me to eat, I wasn't going to open myself up. Just lie there, balled up tight, was all I wanted to do for the rest of my life.

"Reverend Matthews called. He said the whole church is praying for you. Your daddy's out getting more milk at the Quick Pantry. How about unlocking this door and coming in the living room for a family talk when he gets back? Could you do that for me, hon?"

Any other time, I'd do just about anything Mom asked. But now that I was in my shell, I didn't want to come out, especially not for Dad. I needed more time. My mind felt bruised, like my brain had crashed into something too awful to think about. I couldn't talk now.

I was still a roly-poly bug as I listened to Mom click on

the TV in the living room. And the sound of Mitzi's tiny Chihuahua toenails tapping against the floor as she walked across the kitchen. I knew she was headed to the sofa to sit with Mom.

I rolled over on my back and stared at the dim shapes of the ceiling fan's paddles overhead. Maybe I needed Mom to bring me one of those pills. I wanted to sleep, because when you're asleep, it's like you're nowhere. You don't have to talk to anybody or hear the phone ring . . . or remember things that happened.

I must have dozed off anyway. Next thing I knew, the grandfather clock in the hall chimed eleven times. The echo of the last chime was still in my head when I heard loud banging sounds on my bedroom door.

"Daniel? Open up, son."

Dad's harsh voice hurt my ears. More banging, this time so hard my door shook on its hinges. My stomach churned. For a moment, I thought I might be sick. *Go away, Dad. Go away.*

"I didn't know you'd be at the store so long, Ray. Let Daniel sleep tonight. You can talk in the morning." Mom's voice in the hall.

"*Daniel!* I know you hear me. Get yourself out here right now. Stop acting like a baby."

Dad sounded mean. I could tell he'd done more than get milk at the Quick Pantry. He'd probably gone to Athens for some beers. Why wasn't he all balled up in his bed, grieving over his brother, instead of out drinking? Didn't Dad have any feelings at all, other than hateful ones?

"Daniel, listen to me. Been thinking 'bout what happened

to Clay . . . and how I acted this afternoon. We really need to talk," Dad said in a more normal voice.

Dad waited for me to say something. When I didn't, he cleared his throat and said, "Okay, son. If you ain't coming out, I'm coming in."

"Ray," Mom pleaded.

Next thing I heard was lock-picking noises. Another twist of the tool and Dad would be in my room.

In a sudden burst of energy, I rolled off my bed, dashed across my room to the closet and jerked open the door. Shoving my way through school clothes, I pushed past plastic storage tubs until I got to the back wall.

What now? My breaths came out in ragged huffs as I listened to Dad tromp across my room. Nowhere to go but up. I shoved a couple of plastic tubs under the attic opening, pushed open the trapdoor, and hoisted myself up into the darkness.

chaptersix

I grabbed at air until I got lucky and caught hold of the
string, yanking it down and turning on the light. While my
eyes adjusted to the glaring brightness, I heard Dad below,
stumbling through my closet.

Then his muffled words, "What you think you're doing
up there?"

What was I doing up here? Leaning my head against a
wooden rafter near the door, I breathed in the familiar
mustiness and hugged myself tight. I was a roly-poly bug
again, all closed up and safe in the attic.

Safe? Who was I kidding? In a couple of minutes, Dad
would be up here, talking to me with his beer and tobacco
breath in my face. He said he'd done some thinking. I didn't
believe him.

"Ray, let Daniel rest now. There's no harm in him stay-
ing up in the attic for a while."

Mom's voice. She was in my room. Maybe Dad would back off.

I headed toward the attic door. I needed Mom now, needed one of her warm hugs. Needed her to nuzzle her nose in my hair and talk to me in her soft voice. Maybe if I went back down there, I wouldn't feel so horrible.

"Attic's a funny place to rest," Dad said.

"Ray, really . . . can't you give Daniel a break after what's happened? Remember how you felt after the accident on Hooper Gap?"

"You know I don't talk about that, Melissa," Dad snapped. "How 'bout you help me get Daniel down here, so we can talk about what happened in the woods? He can't spend the rest of his life hiding like some chicken scaredy-cat, 'fraid to even have a conversation with his own daddy."

Some chicken scaredy-cat? Why couldn't Dad just shut his stupid mouth? I beat my fist against the attic door, jamming a splinter right into my index finger.

"*Ouch!*" I sucked at the bleeding spot, thankful the color didn't show up in the dim attic light. Blood was something I didn't ever want to see again.

"I hear you beating on that door, son. Get yourself down here right now!" Dad shouted. I'm counting to three. One . . . two . . ."

No way was I going down there to talk about the accident. I didn't want Dad to explode. My legs didn't need striping. I wasn't a rocking chair for him to throw around.

"Three!" Dad shouted. I felt the attic door move beneath me as he tried to push it open.

Plain old Daniel couldn't get out of this jam. It was time

for D-Man to make an appearance. I summoned all my superhero strength and shouted, "Back off, Dad! I'm sleeping in the attic tonight."

"You ain't doing no such thing!" Dad yelled back. I felt myself rise in the air, then fall as Dad shoved the door harder.

"What's wrong with Daniel sleeping up there tonight, Ray?" Mom was trying to make her voice sound calm. But I heard her nervousness.

The door beneath me stopped moving. It seemed like a very long time before Dad said anything. When he spoke, his words surprised me. "Stay up there if you want to—but just tonight. I want you down here in the morning."

I listened to Mom's and Dad's footsteps as they left my room, talking in low voices I couldn't understand. Then I walked over to the far side of the attic, near the windows. Clay and I liked to come up here on rainy days and read comics, so there were plenty of those scattered around. Spawn, the Amazing Spider-Man, Green Hornet, Masked Avenger, Superman. We liked them all.

I ran my hand across a Superman comic, tracing the big red S on Superman's chest with my finger, thinking about how Clay's hand had probably been the last one to touch that shiny cover before tonight.

I felt a sudden flash of anger. Clay was gone. He'd never touch a comic book or call me D-Man, or even Daniel, again.

It wasn't fair, I thought, flinging the comic across the attic, making its brittle pages flap like wings. If Clay couldn't read a Superman comic, I didn't want to either. I was hurting tonight. Big-time. More than I ever had in my life. I didn't know if I'd ever read a comic again.

I stared wild-eyed at all the dusty junk around me. Antique trunk. Broken kitchen chairs. Dad's army duffel bag full of green clothes he called fatigues. My heart beat paradiddles, like I was all revved up. At the same time, I felt so tired. No way could I get any rest up here. What was I thinking?

I crept back to the attic door and listened to my parents argue their way through the house. Living room. Kitchen. Living room again. Down the hall. And finally into their bedroom, where someone—probably Dad—slammed the door.

After a while, the house got quiet. Maybe Mom and Dad wouldn't hear me if I went back down to my room now. I opened the door and dropped onto the plastic tubs in my closet.

Back in my room, I tiptoed to the door and peered out into the hallway. Their bedroom door was still closed. I could hear the muffled sounds of Dad's long-winded snores. I hoped Mom was asleep, too, and Mitzi, as I slipped into the bathroom to relieve myself, then sneaked into the kitchen to answer my growling stomach.

Cool air puffed against my face as I opened the refrigerator and admired the chicken and dumplings. Little lumps of white chicken meat and dough balls floating in a Tupperware bowl of golden broth.

My mouth watered as I popped open the plastic top and dug my fingers into the cold stew. Cramming a chilly dumpling into my mouth, I felt its soft dough walls collapse as I swallowed it.

Back in my room, I stared at my bed with the quilt all rumpled and the pillows tossed around. I wanted to go there. To sink down into those soft bedcovers. To sleep and sleep and sleep.

But how could I climb into my bed and sleep like nothing bad had happened? It didn't matter how tired I felt. Clay wasn't in his bed tonight. He was dead. Dead because of me and my stupid carelessness. And he was never coming back. *Never.*

I didn't deserve to sleep in my comfortable bed tonight. And no way did I want to talk to Dad in the morning. He'd just lose his temper and get all ugly and I didn't need that.

I walked to the window and stood there watching the trees in our yard wave this way and that in the night breeze. The moon, fat and silvery, stared back at me like some giant's eye. Some giant who knew what had happened when Clay and I went hunting. Some lumberjack giant who had stood there, towering over the treetops, watching the rabbit, watching the gun, watching the whole thing without trying to stop it.

Shivering, I thought about that shotgun sound in the woods. *Boom!* Clay slumping to his knees. Falling on his face in the pine straw. Blood spreading on his jacket when I turned him over. The vacant stare in his blue eyes. No kid should ever have to see a look like that.

I sucked in my breath and tried to stop myself from trembling. Was I really a coward like Dad said? A chicken scaredy-cat? A boy who couldn't even talk to his dad about what he'd done? A stupid baby who couldn't hold his gun steady? A kid who shot his own uncle instead of a rabbit?

I looked through the window again. This time I strained to see Sartain Woods in the distance. Dark. Ominous. Monster trees swaying in the night wind. I used to like the woods. Now they were a scary place. A place where terrible things happened. Where someone you loved could walk down a pine-straw-covered path and never come back.

I didn't ever want to walk in those woods again. But I didn't want to be in this house tonight with Dad, either. Dad who might throw a precious chair and break it to pieces. Dad who talked in a hateful voice. Dad who didn't care how much I hurt or how bad I felt.

Maybe I needed to go back to the woods tonight. Maybe that was where I belonged.

Was I afraid? Afraid to go back to that place where Clay went down? Was I really a coward like Dad said?

Was I?

I sucked in my breath and tried to steady myself as I stared at the window latch. Stared at it until I worked up the nerve to extend my hand, to touch the cold brass lock with my trembling fingers and twist it open. I grimaced at the cracking noise as I lifted the window until there was enough space for me to bust through the screen.

Swinging my legs up and over, I dropped to the ground and took off running in my suede bedroom moccasins. My lungs filled with chilly air as I sprinted across our front yard, skidding on the frosty grass. I stumbled down our rutted driveway and staggered onto the dark pavement of Mouse Creek Road, breathing hard.

No cars in sight. Just me, Daniel Sartain, slapping my moccasins against the pavement as I ran. Cold as it was, sweat popped out on my face and in the caves of my underarms as I ran harder and faster than I'd ever run before.

At the meadow, I stopped and doubled over, my hot breaths puffing little steam clouds into the cold darkness. My eyelashes felt like icicles as I stared into the woods at the meadow's edge. It was so dark it'd take Superman's secret X-ray vision just to figure out where the path started.

A panicky feeling grabbed my insides. I glanced back at our white frame house in the distance. A cozy cottage, Mom called it. Nestled on a hill with frosty pines and hardwoods stretching all around it toward the sky.

Maybe I should go back. The thin cloth of my pajamas wasn't going to keep me warm out here. I might even freeze if I stayed in the cold woods tonight.

Anyway, things might look different in the morning. That was what Mom always said. Sometimes she was right, though I felt so bad tonight I didn't have much hope of that being true.

I was almost back to our driveway, panting and trying to catch my breath, when the attic light blinked on.

Dad was in the attic? Sucking in my breath, I turned around and bolted back toward the woods.

chapterseven

The woods took me in, hiding me in pine-scented darkness as I ran, my moccasins crunching pinecones on the path, my ears full of night sounds from unseen animals.

After a while, I had to stop. Panting hard and hugging myself to keep warm, I strained my eyes, trying to see where I was. All around me, trees swayed, making soft sounds in the air, like they were breathing.

Somewhere up ahead, something—maybe an owl—screeched. The hairs on the back of my neck bristled. Maybe I should go back to the house.

Mom was off for a whole week. She'd be home in the morning, making me a real breakfast instead of those frozen waffles I usually ate. Pancakes and grits with lots of butter. Maybe she'd never go back to work.

No. Dad was in the attic, getting all mad because he couldn't find me. I couldn't go back now.

I cupped my face with my hands and rubbed my cheeks, trying to warm them. My hot breath puffed white clouds into the cold night air as I tried not to shake.

This was just the woods, I told myself. Sartain land as far as I could see in every direction. Nothing to be afraid of. Nothing to worry about. I was a Sartain, at least on the outside.

But in my whole life, I'd never been out in these woods without Uncle Clay. He'd always been here, showing me how to make fire by rubbing a dry stick and tinder together real fast. Telling me which berries were good to eat and which were poisonous.

Warning me about danger.

"Watch out, D-Man!" Clay had shouted once as I rounded a curve in the path near the lake. I'd almost stepped on a big grayish snake, curled with its flat head and snake eyes pointed at me, tongue darting in and out of its mouth.

"Timber rattler. See those black cross-bands? Best thing to do is back away. He won't bother you if you don't bother him," Clay said.

I shivered, hugging myself tighter, trying not to feel so cold and scared. Were timber rattlers out this time of year? In these woods? At night? Slithering under cover of darkness up the pine-straw path? Or curled ready to strike when I walked around the next bend?

Maybe they were all hibernating in their burrows. Huddled together underground. Waiting out the winter.

By the calendar, it wasn't officially winter, even though it felt cold enough. It was just November twenty-third— or maybe the twenty-fourth if it was past midnight now.

Winter didn't officially start until December twenty-first. Did snakes follow the calendar? What if snakes hadn't gone underground yet? Who was going to warn me now? Now that Clay was gone?

A chilly night breeze rippled through tree branches overhead, making me shiver more as I took off running, thinking about those snakes underground—or not. Thinking about Clay on the ground, bleeding. Wondering where he was now.

Mom had said they were doing an autopsy. How long would that take? I couldn't stop myself from imagining Clay in some cold room, on a metal table. I'd seen something like that on *Doogie Howser* once. They cut that guy open and looked at his insides.

But they were only cutting Clay's body, right? Wasn't his spirit somewhere else? Like out in the woods with me tonight? Maybe that was what I heard in the trees—those breathing sounds all around me. Maybe Clay's spirit would keep me safe. From the snakes. And the freezing cold. Even from Dad.

Knowing Dad, he'd be out here soon, chasing me through the woods like I was some runaway rabbit. He might even have his belt off so he could teach me another one of his lessons. *Crack!* I could hear him snapping that leather. Like it was a whip and I was a circus animal he was trying to tame.

D-Man wouldn't put up with Dad's meanness. He'd fight him. I tried to feel like D-Man as I ran on through the woods. But I wasn't even sure if I was heading in the right direction.

After a while, my chest hurt so bad I had to stop running again. Breathing hard, I rested a minute, staring up through the dark trees. My mouth felt like a wad of dirty cotton as I watched a cloud drift across the moon.

I knew where I was now. I wasn't anywhere near the accident site. I was way on the other side of the woods—not too far from Clay's cabin. But I couldn't go there without Clay.

When my breathing had calmed down to normal speed, I started running again, moving through the trees, listening for Dad sounds behind me. *Concentrate, D-Man,* Clay would say. *Pay attention. Listen for Ray.*

I didn't hear any Dad sounds as I ran on through the woods, just the soft patting of my moccasins against the straw. And the peeps of unseen birds nearby. Yips of a far-away coyote. And breathing, a soft brushing together of tree limbs in the night breeze.

Why hadn't I just killed the rabbit instead of my uncle? *Boom!* I imagined the cartridge exploding out the barrel of my .410, releasing pellets into the air. Striking the soft gray-brown fur of that stupid, frozen rabbit. Blood spurting.

"Way to go, D-Man. Perfect shot!" Clay would have shouted, dancing a happy dance in his camouflage boots, pulling off his cap and tossing it in the air. Holding up that bloody rabbit like it was a grand prize, a great accomplishment for D-Man, boy superhero.

Somewhere behind me, I heard a noise like the snapping of a twig. I pushed my tired legs to run faster, but it didn't matter how fast I ran. Something—or someone—behind me was getting closer.

A cough, then a voice: "Daniel?"

Dad. Glancing back over my shoulder, I tried to see him. He wasn't close enough yet. But any minute, he'd catch up with me.

I gulped in a deep breath of air and turned back toward Clay's cabin, taking a roundabout route. I hadn't planned on going there, but what else could I do with Dad so close behind me?

"Wait up, son!" Dad shouted in a wheezy voice.

Was he crazy? No way was I waiting. I was already way ahead of Dad, pumping my legs and running hard as I could. The more he yelled at me to wait, to stop, the faster I ran.

A couple of minutes later, Clay's dark cabin came into view in the moonlight, a rough-hewn log house with a wide front porch.

Dad had almost caught up with me then, breathing so hard I thought he might collapse as his boots crunched on Clay's gravel driveway.

I scrambled toward the porch steps.

"You can't go in there—cabin's locked tight," Dad sputtered as he slumped against Clay's black pickup, trying to catch his breath. His dark outline in the moonlight looked so much like Clay, I felt like I ought to stop and run back to him—until I remembered who he really was.

"Cabin's all mine now. Everything in it and Clay's half of the land. You got no business in there."

"I can go in there if I want to!" I shouted, feeling like D-Man for a moment as my hot words exploded into the cold night air, launching like torpedoes right into Dad's greedy face. He might look like an older version of Clay, but he wouldn't ever be Clay.

"Watch how you talk to me, son. You ought not to be out here. Come on home. Get some rest." Dad coughed a tight, choking cough as he limped toward me.

"You're the one who needs rest," I said, darting toward the steps and pulling a key out of its hiding place.

Clay called it the emergency key. *"For when I'm somewhere else and you want to be in the cabin,"* he'd told me the day he hid the key in that nook underneath the top step. He didn't say, *"For when you need to get away from your dad."* But I figured that was what Clay meant, because he knew all about Dad's explosive temper.

Dad coughed again as he moved closer.

With the key in my hand, I dashed around to the back of the cabin and sprinted up the wooden steps with Dad right behind me. I jerked open the screen door and jabbed the key at the lock.

It wouldn't go in.

Panicking, I glanced back over my shoulder. Dad had stopped on the porch, trying to catch his breath. He was holding his side again, like it really hurt.

I twisted the key around and stuck it into the lock. This time it fit. I was already in Clay's dark kitchen, with the door locked behind me, before Dad even caught on to what I was doing.

"This ain't funny, Daniel. Open the door." Dad rapped on the door glass. "Let me talk to you."

Dad had decided we were going to talk. No matter what I did, he'd keep on until I let him in.

But I was stubborn, too. Dad could just stay out there. I didn't ask him to come after me. He was the one who needed to go back to the house. Go back and drink a six-pack of beer, smoke a whole pack of stinky cigarettes.

What I needed was right here in this cabin. I could sleep on Clay's sofa tonight, like I had so many times before. Smelling his smell, breathing in the air he'd breathed. Surrounded by his things.

I had memories of this cabin. When Dad was drinking—storming around our house, yelling and screaming until nobody could stand him—that was when Mom would bundle me up and bring me here.

"Stay," Clay would say to both of us. *"You don't have to listen to Ray rant. Melissa, you really ought to think about taking Daniel and going back to Soddy-Daisy. I'd miss both of you something terrible, but that's what I'd do, if I were you."*

But Mom never stayed with us. She always went home, saying she and Dad had to talk things out. I felt so scared for Mom when she did that. Each time we waited for Mom to come back, I wished Clay were my dad, even though he was only twelve when I was born and Mom called him the little brother she never had.

"Daniel, let me in!" Dad yelled, banging on the door.

"Not by the hair of my chinny-chin-chin!" I yelled back, remembering a bedtime story Clay used to read on those nights when I camped out in his cabin. Us all bundled up on the couch under one of Grandmama's quilts. A fire crackling in the fireplace. Clay reading a story in his deep voice from one of those books he got for Christmas when he was a kid.

"Daniel? You're acting like a two-year-old brat."

Tonight, Dad was the Big Bad Wolf. And I was the little piggy who wasn't going to let him into my house of wood. He'd just have to go away.

Dad hadn't said anything for a while. Had he gone back home? Easing up to the window beside the door, I looked out. He wasn't on the porch.

"Daniel?"

Dad's muffled voice came from the front door now. The doorknob rattled as he tried to force his way in. When that didn't work, he said, "Tell you what, son. You don't have to open this door. Just listen to me . . . *please?* That's all I'm asking."

Please? Dad had never said *please* to me before, not that I could remember. It was one of those words that weren't in his vocabulary, like *thanks*, *sorry*, and *love*. Dad was full of nasty words that stank as bad as those endless cigarette-smoke clouds he wheezed out into the world.

"If I stop talking, how 'bout you throw me one of Mama's old quilts? So your old man don't freeze to death. Okay?"

I didn't answer. Turning away from the door, I closed my eyes and leaned back against the log wall, feeling its roughness through my pajama shirt. I didn't want Dad to freeze, but no way was I opening the door to toss him anything.

"You awake in there?" Dad's voice had a hateful tone now.

When I still didn't answer, Dad pressed his face against the glass, peering in at me like I was locked away somewhere in an uncle-killer jail and he had come to visit.

"I'm listening to you," I snapped.

"Made the arrangements for Clay at Morgan's Funeral

Home today," Dad said. "Did you know the game warden—Nick—is in charge of the investigation? Thought it'd be the sheriff. That place where Clay got shot . . . it's a crime scene until Nick rules it an accident and closes the case."

Of course I knew. I'd never forget the circle of yellow plastic crime-scene tape in the woods with those endless black letters: "Crime Scene Do Not Cross."

"Can't have Clay's funeral till the body comes back from the crime lab in Decatur. They'll have test results any day. Then they'll know if what you told 'em at the site is true."

I knew what I'd said was true. But what if the tests said something else? I shivered as I thought about what might happen then. Bad kids got sent to a detention center near Atlanta. I'd heard it was worse than jail.

"Went ahead and picked out a casket and the flowers and . . . Daniel, you listening to me?"

"Yeah, Dad." I was listening, even though my ears didn't want to hear what Dad was saying. He was trying to talk nice, but every word about the crime-lab tests and the funeral arrangements hurt, like Dad was slapping the sounds into my ears.

"Did everything but pick out a date for Clay's service."

Why was Dad telling me all this grown-up stuff? I felt shaky as a vision of Clay stretched out in a coffin popped into my mind. Big, strong, full-of-life Clay stuck in the ground forevermore. With wrinkled old Grandmama and Granddaddy Sartain and all the other dead bodies in our family cemetery.

Clay shouldn't be there. But he would be soon. All because of me.

The more I thought about that, the more I wanted to hit something. Hard. Instead, I hugged myself tight and tried to choke back the sick feelings churning in my stomach. Clay was dead and it was all my fault. Why hadn't I shot the stupid rabbit instead? How would I ever be able to go to the funeral? Or do anything else in my life? Why couldn't Dad just shut up?

I had to stop Dad from talking. It didn't matter if he was talking polite or hateful now, or somewhere in between. Each word he said blistered me. I couldn't listen to those hurting words anymore.

So I opened the door.

chaptereight

Dad didn't say anything at first. We just looked, him on the porch and me in the doorway, studying each other's faces in the moonlight. Dad's face looked worried, with those lines on his forehead deeper than I'd ever seen them before.

I don't know what Dad saw when he looked at me. Maybe he saw an eleven-year-old boy with lines on his forehead, too. A sad kid who had shot his beloved uncle and would never be the same.

Dad coughed. He cleared his throat and stepped inside. The moonlight outside streamed in through the cabin windows, giving everything a ghostly glow. I watched Dad look all around his brother's cabin—the home he knew so well from living here himself when he was a kid—like he hadn't ever seen this place before.

When he'd looked enough, Dad reached over and flipped on the overhead light.

The explosion of brightness made my eyes blink and hurt. They got all watery as I looked at Clay's things. Brown vinyl recliner. Plaid couch. The big rock fireplace with a stack of logs and a basket of tinder on the hearth, waiting for someone to start a fire.

Dad cleared his throat. Twice. He dug his fingers into the pocket of his flannel shirt and pulled out a cigarette and a red plastic lighter. He flipped the lighter top and it ignited a tiny, flickering flame.

The round cigarette end caught fire, and I stepped back as a cloud of nasty-smelling smoke drifted toward me. I wanted to tell Dad that this would be a good time to quit smoking and that would be a really good way to honor Clay.

Instead, I blurted, "Hope you got Clay a good casket," like I was all grown up instead of just an eleven-year-old boy.

"Did. Polished oak like your granddaddy Sartain's," Dad answered with smoke streaming out his nose.

"Good."

Dad puffed on his cigarette like he couldn't finish it fast enough. He stared hard at me with Sartain blue eyes, just like Clay's except for the cold expression. "Game warden filled me in on everything. But I want you to tell me what happened. How come you didn't just shoot the rabbit?"

I swallowed and thought a minute, trying to come up with a good answer to Dad's question. I didn't want to tell him the real reason I didn't shoot the rabbit. He'd call me a chicken scaredy-cat for sure. So I said, "It ran away."

"It ran away." Dad inhaled again. He blew out a stream

of little blue smoke circles and watched them melt into the air. Then he looked at me and blinked his eyes, like he was trying to hold back something.

"I didn't mean for the gun to go off like that, Dad. It was a mistake. A *stupid* mistake. The rabbit ran away. I was getting up from the kneeling position Clay showed me, so I could keep the gun steady while I aimed. We were going to walk on and find another rabbit. But the gun . . . the gun slanted across my chest. And went off."

I took a deep breath of smoky air and tried to stop shaking. "I miss Clay so much."

All the blood drained out of Dad's face as he stared into my eyes, inhaling cigarette smoke like he could never get enough.

I wanted him to stop looking at me like he could see right into my head and read my thoughts. I didn't want Dad knowing what I was thinking. Why had I said all those words to him just now?

Dad turned his eyes away. "I miss Clay, too, you know," he said, sinking into Clay's recliner. Puffing on his cigarette, he stared at the stack of logs in Clay's fireplace until his face contorted into a frightened expression that scared me.

I started backing away, toward the door, thinking this might be a good time to go home—before Dad got all mean again.

Dad's words stopped me.

"Been pretending I didn't have nothing to feel guilty about for years, Daniel. But all the pretending in the world can't get rid of my guilt. It's always there, eatin' at me." Dad exhaled more smoke rings and watched them float toward the hearth.

What was Dad talking about? I didn't think he felt guilty about anything. Drinking. Smoking. The mean way he treated us.

"You know that accident? The one that killed your granddaddy and grandmama over on Hooper Gap?" Dad looked at me with watery eyes.

I nodded.

"You weren't but 'bout five or six when that happened. Probably don't remember much 'bout the wreck or your grandparents."

"I was six, Dad. And I remember Granddaddy taking me fishing that summer. And Grandmama showed me how to play this card game called Rook. I beat her twice."

"Yeah, Mama and her Rook games. And Pop always tryin' to land that whopper catfish in our lake." Dad's lips twisted until they almost smiled.

Then his face darkened. He took three more quick puffs on his cigarette, coughing smoke. He put the cigarette out in a metal coaster on the lamp table. He got up and walked over to me.

"You wouldn't know I was driving Pop's pickup that day. When the deer ran 'cross the road in front of us. And I swerved to keep from hitting it. And the truck skidded off the road and crashed into the tree."

"Why didn't you tell me, Dad?"

"We decided not to talk about it. Like we could get past it if we didn't say the words. Clay was only seventeen and still livin' at home with Mama and Pop in this cabin when it happened. Guess it was hardest on him. He coulda come live with us. We'da made room for him. But he stayed here. Lady from the county child welfare office let him stay cause he was almost eighteen. And we was close by if he needed anything."

"You should have told me you were driving—"

"Kinda thing you try to forget, son. One minute your folks are in the truck with you. Mama laughing and talking 'bout that mess of pole beans she's gonna pick in the garden when she gets home. Pop tellin' me we're going fishing the next morning."

Dad turned his eyes away. He shuddered.

I knew he was remembering the accident scene—like I remembered Clay in the woods. I wondered if he'd seen his mama and daddy dead . . . if he'd seen blood.

"Were you hurt in that wreck, Dad?"

"Where you think I got my limp? And my head—it ain't never been right since. Can't think straight. Can't work."

"Weren't y'all wearing seat belts?"

"Wore mine. But your grandparents didn't believe in 'em."

"Were you drunk, Dad? Were you driving drunk that day?" I felt the blood rush to my face as I thought about Dad's drinking habit.

Dad shook his head. "No, son. Didn't start drinking till after Mama and Pop died. I felt so bad 'bout what happened. Nothing mattered to me then 'cep' finding a way to stop remembering."

Dad turned back to the fireplace. I heard him sobbing.

"What happened out there in the woods . . . to Clay . . . that made me do some more thinkin' 'bout that wreck on Hooper Gap," Dad said.

"What do you mean?"

Dad turned around and looked at me with a pained expression. "Been blaming that deer all these years. But *I* was driving when that animal darted 'cross Hooper Gap. *I* shoulda been able to control the truck."

Dad hung his head. He slumped into the recliner and put his hands over his face.

"You all right, Dad? What happened to Grandmama and Granddaddy wasn't your fault. It was an accident. Mr. Hooper told me accidents happen, when he was bringing me home that day after Clay went down. He said we just have to deal with them."

But not by turning into a drunk, I thought.

And then something really scary came into my head. I saw myself grown up like Dad, drinking beers and smoking cigarettes. Picking up somebody's favorite chair and smashing it against a wall. Striping a little boy's legs with my belt. Keeping my mouth in a mean, straight line.

I was going to end up just like Dad. And I didn't know how I was going to live with that.

After a while, Dad got control of himself. He lit another cigarette and sat there a long time, inhaling smoke, then letting it curl out into the air, adding more stinky tobacco smells to the cabin.

"There's a patch for that," Clay would say whenever Dad lit up around him. "Can't you quit, big brother? You know all that nicotine is rotting out your lungs."

"When you get perfect, you can tell me what to do, baby brother," Dad would answer.

All that guilt over his parents' accident—that guilt Dad felt, but pretended he didn't—had changed him. Changed him into a monster. Was I going to change into a monster like that? Some creepy comic-book villain like Lex Luthor?

Dad got up. He snuffed out his cigarette, then turned back and looked at me like he was going to say something.

Before he could get the words out of his mouth, we heard wheels crunching gravel outside. Through the windows, I saw headlights beam across the yard. The car door opened and Mom got out and rushed up the steps.

She rapped on the door glass. "Daniel? Ray?"

I opened the door and Mom pulled me into her arms, hugging me so tight it almost hurt.

"I woke up and you were both gone," she said. "I couldn't think of anywhere else to look but here." I felt Mom's heart beating against my face and smelled her talcum powder.

"Ray, you okay?" Mom loosened her grip on me and looked over at Dad.

Dad nodded, staring at the unlit logs in Clay's fireplace.

"Come on," Mom said, herding us both toward the door. "Get in the car. We're going back to the house. We all need some sleep. Game warden's coming by tomorrow with the autopsy results."

chapternine

The next morning, I heard Mom in the kitchen as I walked down the hall to the bathroom. Any other Wednesday morning she would be at work and I'd be getting ready for school—hurrying to dress and eat breakfast before the bus got here.

Today I wasn't going anywhere, I thought, flushing the commode and watching the water swirl round and round as it gurgled out of sight. And that was okay with me. I couldn't imagine getting on a bus full of kids' staring faces.

"You must be hungry," Mom said, handing me a plate of pancakes as I slid into my seat at the table. Pancakes were my favorite breakfast, but today the smell of them made me sick.

Mom brought her coffee to the table and sat across from me. She took quick sips from the steaming mug and waited for me to start eating.

I didn't want to disappoint her, so I cut into the stack of pancakes with my fork and shoved a bite into my mouth. The maple syrup tasted so sweet I wanted to spit out my food. But Mom was watching, so I chewed the pancake and washed it down with a big gulp of milk.

"Nicole called a few minutes ago, to see how you were feeling. She said she misses you, and so does Eric," Mom said.

I nodded and tried to eat another bite of pancake. The twins, Nicole and Eric, lived near the intersection of Mouse Creek and Hooper Gap roads, not far from our house. We'd been friends since kindergarten. Of all the kids in my fifth-grade class at Newtonville Elementary, they were the only ones I missed.

"Got your daddy to bring those comics down from the attic yesterday. They're in your room. Thought you might want to do some reading," Mom said.

"Thanks." I'd noticed the boxes by my bookcase. I looked at Mom drinking her coffee and I wanted to talk to her about what Dad had told me last night at Clay's cabin. But I couldn't make the words come out of my mouth.

The rest of the morning went by in a blur as Mom and I huddled together on the sofa watching videos on the VCR. I can't remember the names or anything that happened in those movies. I guess I watched them with my eyes, but not my mind.

Dad stayed out in the garage most of the day, working on his truck. A little after three, the game warden came by our house. His head brushed the doorframe as he walked in, holding an important-looking envelope in his hand.

"Make yourself at home, Mr. Fortson," Mom said.

The back door opened and Dad walked in, wiping his hands on a greasy shop rag. He nodded at the game warden and the tall man nodded back.

Mr. Fortson sat in Mom's rocker. He opened the envelope and handed Dad an official-looking document.

Dad squinted his eyes as he studied the top page.

While Dad read, moving his lips as he tried to sound out each word, the game warden talked to me. "Basically, what it says, Daniel, is that the state crime-lab reports from the autopsy and the gun tests confirm that your uncle died accidentally."

Mr. Fortson looked at Dad again, and Mom; then he turned back to me. "The sheriff and I agree that you didn't mean to shoot your gun that day. But your cartridge fired and caused your uncle's unfortunate death. You folks can go ahead and have the funeral now. My deepest sympathy is with you and your family."

My gun's cartridge. The game warden made it sound like my gun's cartridge had a mind of its own. Like that little black cylinder had launched itself through the barrel of my .410, ending the life of my favorite person in the world—other than Mom. The more I thought about that, the worse I felt.

Shotgun cartridges don't have minds of their own. My gun's cartridge had been in my gun. And my gun had been in my hands. And my finger had nudged the trigger as I got up. It wasn't my cartridge's fault that my uncle was dead. It was *my* fault. I was the killer.

Mom got up and walked into the kitchen and leaned her

head against the refrigerator. I heard her sniffling, like she was reliving last Saturday all over again.

I fell back on the sofa and closed my eyes, trying to shut everything out. The strong smell of smoke made me open my eyes. Dad was pacing the floor and puffing his cigarette all over our living room, his hands all jittery as they moved back and forth to his mouth.

The game warden coughed and shifted in the chair. The chair tried to rock but he stopped it with his long legs.

For once in my life, I was in a room of grown-ups who didn't seem to know what to say. I didn't know what to say, either. So I kept quiet and tried to pretend that I hadn't killed Clay. If I pretended hard enough, maybe the terrible guilt I felt would go away.

"Family counseling might be something to consider," Mr. Fortson said, breaking the silence as he looked over at Dad.

Dad turned his eyes away and puffed out more smoke while Mom nodded from the kitchen, where she was pouring tea into glasses filled with ice cubes. She handed me a glass of iced tea, then gave one to Mr. Fortson.

The game warden sipped tea, nodding his approval at Mom. He looked at me. I couldn't tell what he was thinking. He had one of those official-looking grown-up faces that didn't give hints.

"Daniel, you need to head on back to school as soon as you can. You don't want to get behind with your schoolwork. Get on with your life. I know this is awful for you, but that's the best thing to do," Mr. Fortson said.

Get on with my life? I imagined myself walking into my

fifth-grade classroom at Newtonville Elementary, with all the kids' eyes boring into me like daggers. Looking at me like I was some freak. Some monster kid who had killed his uncle. I couldn't go back to school.

Mr. Fortson handed Dad a copy of the accident report. He thanked Mom for the tea, then headed out the door to his forest green pickup with Dad walking beside him.

I stood at the living room window, watching as the game warden popped open the truck's tailgate. He pulled out a long, narrow package and handed it to Dad.

Dad shook his head and walked to the garage, holding the package out in front of him like it was on fire. I knew he had my .410.

After the game warden drove away, Dad came back in the house without the gun.

"Game warden brought the shotgun back," he said, turning on the water faucet in the kitchen. He scrubbed his hands a long time, then rinsed them over and over. "I hid it in a safe place."

"There isn't a safe place for something like that, Ray," Mom said.

Dad nodded and dried his hands on the dish towel hanging by the sink. Then he spent a long time staring out the window. I knew he was looking at the garage.

That night in bed, I couldn't stop thinking about my .410. Polished walnut stock. Long black barrel. Tiny silver sight-post gleaming at the end. Each time I got close to sleep, I felt that gun, heavy and dangerous in my hands as my finger curled against the trigger.

Boom! I heard the awful noise over and over in my head. And I saw Clay falling.

I sat up, rubbing my eyes, glancing around at the darkness. I knew Dad had hidden my gun in the garage. And I had to find the .410. So I could throw it in the lake, like I wanted to that day in the woods. Maybe then I could forget about my shotgun. Maybe then I wouldn't hurt so bad.

chapterten

Mom pulled containers of food from Newtonville Deli out of a sack. She lined them up across the kitchen counter, like pieces in a puzzle, and studied everything.

"Works for me," she said, peeking beneath a tinfoil cover at a very flat pumpkin pie. How about you, Daniel?"

"Same here," I said as Mom unearthed a small tin of dressing and a dry-looking turkey with several charred spots near its legs.

If I'd been really hungry, like I'd been every other Thanksgiving I could remember, I'd be worried about our food. But I didn't feel hungry, or sad that I wasn't hungry, or full of thanks for anything. Truth was, it didn't matter if we ever had Thanksgiving again. I didn't care.

"Well." Mom pursed her lips and picked at the charred spots. "Wonder what Ray will say about this Thanksgiving feast? Ah, let's not worry about that today. We didn't have to cook our food. And cleanup will be a snap, right, hon?"

"Right," I agreed, feeling thankful that the meal looked so bad nobody would care if I didn't eat more than two bites. The old Daniel would be worried about Dad's reaction to our store-bought meal. But today, it didn't matter. It wasn't really Thanksgiving if you didn't have anything to be thankful about.

"How about you set the table while I get this food warmed up," Mom said, trying to make her voice sound cheerful.

"Yes, ma'am."

Mom popped the turkey in the microwave first. I was surprised by how good it smelled.

Our house was so small that we didn't have a separate dining room. So our china cabinet was wedged into a corner of the kitchen near the laundry room. I pulled open the glass doors, took out the Currier & Ives dinner plates, and hauled them to the table.

"Careful with those," Mom said, glancing back at me from the microwave.

We always ate our Thanksgiving meal on these plates with their colorful, old-fashioned scenes. Mom inherited the set from Grandmama Russell. But we only had three plates now because last year I dropped one, breaking it into a million pieces.

Each plate had a different scene. My favorite was "A Home in the Wilderness." I put that one in Mom's place, centering it on the lacy white tablecloth. I liked the log cabin with smoke puffing out the chimney. And the antique mom feeding chickens with the little girl beside her. And the horse, or was that a mule?

I'd never looked at our Currier & Ives plates this closely before. The horse—it was a horse—had a dead animal strapped across its back—a deer maybe. And beside the horse walked a boy about my age. And a man with a gun. I could see they'd been hunting.

I sucked in my breath, listening to the hum of the microwave, and tried not to think hunting thoughts as I placed a plate with another scene, "The Old Homestead in Winter," in Dad's place. We didn't get much snow in Georgia. But at least this snow-scene plate didn't make me think about killing things.

I placed "The Homestead in Winter" plate in my place. This plate showed a newer homestead with a bigger house and a horse-drawn sleigh.

"Table looks nice," Mom said, brushing past me on her way to the refrigerator. "Can you believe it? I almost forgot the cranberry sauce. Can't have Thanksgiving dinner without that."

I made my lips smile at Mom as she scooted back by me, holding the Tupperware container; then I turned back to the table. There was still one more place left to set. Ever since my grandparents died, Clay had eaten Thanksgiving dinner with us. Should I set his place today? I wondered if it would feel worse to leave the spot empty or fill it with a plate.

A plate would be better, I decided, going back to the china cabinet. Even though I'd broken one of the plates we'd always used, there were other sets—stacked in neat rows and propped up for display.

On one end, I found a different Currier & Ives plate, from the American Sportsman series. Perfect, I thought, taking it out of the china cabinet and sliding it into Clay's place at the table. The tiny man dressed in buckskins, sitting in the canoe, looked just like him.

"*Good choice, D-Man,*" Clay's voice whispered in my head as I added glasses and silverware. "*I knew you wouldn't forget me.*"

I watched Mom pull the last container of deli food out of the microwave: a steaming green bean casserole. It felt weird—hearing Clay's voice in my head. But I liked it. It made me feel like he was really here.

Mom glanced at the table, then over at me with a smile. I couldn't tell if she'd noticed Clay's place setting. It seemed so natural to have his plate and glass and silverware there, maybe she didn't think anything about it.

"Ray, dinner's ready!" Mom shouted toward the bedroom.

I heard Dad making noises in there, like he was bumping into things. Mom had to call him two more times before he finally stumbled into the kitchen. His face had beard stubble and his hair looked wild and uncombed.

Dad squinted at the deli turkey, shaking his head. Mom had set the bird by Dad's plate. She'd placed the electric knife we always used on holidays beside it.

Dad grabbed the knife, then let it drop on the table.

"What kind of turkey is this, Melissa?" Dad poked at one of the charred spots on the pale bird. He looked at Mom and made a gagging sound in his throat. "I know you didn't cook this thing. It's too ugly."

"Newtonville Deli cooked our Thanksgiving dinner this year," Mom explained. "We didn't have to cook a thing."

Dad frowned. "Can't remember the last time I didn't have a home-cooked Thanksgiving dinner. Where's your sweet potato casserole, Melissa? Don't seem like Thanksgiving without sweet potatoes."

I couldn't help agreeing with Dad. I could almost taste the marshmallow topping as I watched Mom take her place at the table. She slapped a big gooey gob of dressing onto her Currier & Ives plate, topping it with a ladle of greenish gray giblet gravy.

"Humph," Dad said, clicking on the electric knife and pointing the shiny metal blade at the turkey. The knife buzzed and whirred as he hacked the bird into a pile of thin, dry slices.

I stared at the turkey meat, wondering how bad it would taste.

"Hey, D-Man. That's one pitiful-looking bird," Clay's voice said. "She don't even look like a turkey. Looks more like an anorexic chicken."

I choked back a tiny giggle as I watched Dad pass the platter of turkey—or was it chicken?—to Mom. She took a few slices, then passed the platter to me.

The heavy brown earthenware wobbled in my hands as I took a slice. I set the platter down by Clay's plate, making his silverware rattle.

My parents' eyes followed the platter and stared at the Sportsman plate, then turned back to their food. Like if they pretended they didn't see Clay's empty plate and chair, they weren't there.

"This turkey tastes funny, you know?" Dad said.

"Tastes okay to me. What do you think, Daniel?" Mom asked, trying to chew the dry meat.

"It's bad," I admitted, dropping a bit of meat under the table for Mitzi. "Bet Clay would agree with that, don't you?"

"What?" Dad looked across the table at the empty plate in Clay's place. He stared at the guy in buckskins for a minute; then something ignited in his eyes. He shot up, making his chair crash behind him to the floor.

"Been trying to ignore that plate, but I can't stand it anymore. What's going on?" Dad demanded, pointing his finger at Clay's place. "We don't set the table for somebody dead. That's crazy."

Mom's lips trembled as she stared at Clay's plate.

"I know you didn't set the table," Dad said, looking at Mom. "That leaves you, son."

I nodded, wondering what Dad was going to do about it. Would he hurl the plate across the room like a Frisbee? Or smash it against the table into a million tiny pieces? Or just throw it in the trash?

"Ray, it's Thanksgiving," Mom said in a soft voice.

By the way Dad was twisting his face and grimacing, I could tell he was thinking about doing something bad. But somehow, he got control of himself. He didn't explode.

Instead, he surprised me when he picked up his chair, sat back down at the table, and cleaned his plate. A couple of times, I saw him staring at the tiny man in buckskins, canoeing across the American Sportsman plate. But he didn't say another word.

For dessert, we ate flat wedges of yellow-orange pumpkin pie with swirls of whipped cream topping. And as we cleared the table, it was Mom who smashed Clay's plate on the hard tile kitchen floor. She wouldn't say if she broke the plate on purpose. But I thought she did. I helped her sweep up the sharp-edged pieces, looking for the Clay-like hunter. But he was gone.

We'd just finished loading the dishwasher when the phone rang.

"That was Mrs. Pettibone," Mom said, hanging up the receiver. "She said not to worry about riding the bus Monday. She's coming by to pick you up for school."

"Call her back and tell her I'm not going," I said.

"I'll do no such thing," Mom said. "I'm going back to work on Sunday night, Daniel. And you're going back to school. I know you're nervous about it, but you have to go."

"I'd take you myself, but looks like you already got yourself a ride," Dad said.

chaptereleven

The day after Thanksgiving, we buried Clay in the dark earth of our family cemetery in Sartain Woods.

Dad had decided we wouldn't have the usual visitation at the funeral home. He said it'd be too hard on us. Mom and I agreed. But it seemed like skipping the wake had made more people come to the graveside service.

Cold air stung my cheeks as I walked to the front row of folding chairs, underneath the canvas funeral-home tent. I tried not to look at all the faces around me. But I felt everyone's eyes boring into me as I sat down.

Mom sat next to me in her Sunday black dress. Dad slid into the chair on my other side, looking uncomfortable in his brown suit that he almost never wore. His new black shoes—they didn't match his suit, Mom had told him, but he'd bought them anyway—tapped against the green Astroturf carpet the funeral-home people had spread over the ground.

Clay would get a big kick out of this tent, I thought, trying not to look at his casket displayed on a metal stand right in front of us. He'd say it looked just like the circus, except for the big Morgan's Funeral Home logos on the sides.

"Don't get comfortable yet," Dad said, catching my arm as I slumped back in the chair and pulling me to my feet. "They're fixing to close the casket so the service can start. Let's go tell Clay goodbye."

"Do we have to?" I wanted Dad to let go of my arm. I wasn't going up there.

"Clay would want you to say goodbye, Daniel," Mom said, getting up from her chair and taking my other arm.

I sighed and walked with Mom and Dad to the casket. I'd already seen Clay dead in the woods. I didn't know if I could take another look. So I turned my head away and stared at the flowers. Roses. Carnations. Prayer plants. More flowers than I'd ever seen in one place.

"You'll be okay, Daniel. Just think of Clay as asleep," Mom said, curling her arm around my shoulder and pulling me closer to the casket.

"Okay." I said the word, but my feet didn't want to move. I wanted to turn around and run back to my chair and get this whole funeral thing over with. But I couldn't do that with Mom and Dad beside me and all those people I knew back there behind us. And Clay waiting in his box for me to say my final goodbye.

While Mom and Dad stared into the casket, I checked out the shiny oak finish on the casket's sides. And the soft white blanket covering the bottom part of Clay. My eyes twitched as they moved higher, to his pale hands, one folded on top of the other.

Clay didn't hold his hands like that. Ever. They were always moving, doing something. Casting a line into the lake. Grabbing his faded red cap. Slapping my back.

"The funeral home did a good job," Mom whispered.

"Yep, he looks so natural. Like he could get up and . . ." Dad coughed and patted the pack of cigarettes hiding in his suit-coat pocket as he stared at his brother.

I looked at Mom. Her eyes were closed. Her lips moved in a silent prayer.

Without thinking, I glanced back at Clay. He didn't look natural to me. Or like he was asleep. He looked dead, his pale lips smiling like he thought this whole funeral thing was a joke.

I couldn't look anymore. I turned and stumbled back to my chair, falling onto the hard metal seat. Clay wasn't in that casket. That was a body. A *dead* body.

For a moment, I thought he might still be on the ground. In the woods. Bleeding. Waiting for me to come back with help.

I watched two black-suited funeral-home men close Clay's casket. Shutting that wooden box seemed so final, I thought as Reverend Matthews started talking in his soft preacher's voice. Talking about Clay like he knew him real well even though Clay hardly ever went to church.

"My church is the great outdoors," Clay would tell me sometimes on our way to the lake to fish on one of those Sunday mornings when Mom let me miss Sunday school.

"The sky and the trees and the air. How can you not worship all of that, D-Man?"

I worshipped the great outdoors. All of it. But mostly, I worshipped Clay. I'd always worshipped him, and wanted to be just like him. The long-legged way he walked. The deep sound of his voice. The way he loved to have fun, even though he was a grown man.

Now he was quiet. Stretched out in his casket, wearing that charcoal gray suit Mom had bought him at JCPenney. He wasn't ever going to fish or hunt or have fun again . . . thanks to me.

"This is your shot, D-Man. Your shot," Clay had said to me out in the woods last Saturday.

But I hadn't taken my shot. My shot had taken Clay. He was gone. Gone from my life. Gone from these woods. Gone from this whole world.

And I wanted to be just like him. Gone. I didn't want to end up a monster like Dad. All eaten up with guilt and so miserable I didn't care what I did or how I made everyone around me feel.

The preacher stopped talking. He gave us all a serious look as he clasped his pink hands together. His black suit coat was buttoned and it puckered like it might pop open at any minute.

Overhead, we heard the honking calls of Canadian geese as they flew in a huge V formation toward the lake, a couple of miles away.

I closed my eyes, trying to hold back tears as the preacher started talking again.

"A life cut short," Reverend Matthews's soft voice said.

I opened my eyes and looked beyond the preacher at patches of blue-gray sky showing through the treetops. I tried to imagine Clay up there, laughing at all the sad people below him in the woods he loved. Doing his imitation of the Amazing Spider-Man. Pumping up his chest, acting like he was swinging from treetop to treetop by strands of web. Telling me, *"Come on up, D-Man. This is fun."*

"Cut short." Reverend Matthews looked up from his notes and focused his sharp blue eyes on me, slicing my thoughts into tiny pieces.

I tried not to look back at the preacher, but he grabbed my eyes with his, holding them hostage with his serious expression.

His narrow pupils said things to me. About death and guilt and God. *"You are the one,"* the preacher's eyes shouted while his mouth said other, nicer things. *"You are the boy who shot your uncle. Dead. And you're going to pay."*

I couldn't take that look. I already felt like the tiniest person in the world. So little that I might just float up into the trees overhead and disappear. At the same time I felt heavy—all weighed down with guilt.

Glancing away at the people crowding around the edges of the tent, I watched two men Clay had worked with at Wal-Mart try not to look at the casket. Like if they didn't see the polished oak box, Clay wasn't really dead. He was just working his shift in the sporting goods department. Helping customers find the right fishing lure or the perfect set of weights. Maybe even a shotgun or rifle.

I shivered in my suit coat.

"Cut short by an unfortunate accident, deep in the heart

of Sartain Woods." The preacher looked at me again, giving me the willies. He cleared his throat and talked more about Clay's short life.

A wrinkled man in a green suit and two women with matching silver hair and black church clothes stood next to the Wal-Mart guys. And behind them our neighbors, Frank Hooper and his wife, Della; the Fortsons; and the Martins, Eric and Nicole and their parents.

I couldn't help wondering what Clay would have thought about all of this. The casket. The preacher. Us.

"You are one sad-looking kid," Clay's voice whispered in my head. *"Get ahold of yourself, D-Man."*

I wanted to get ahold of myself. I really did. But how could I, listening to Reverend Matthews, sitting here on this hard chair in a scratchy suit that didn't fit right anymore? A tight suit with sleeves that stopped too soon, leaving the skin right above my wrists exposed.

I let my eyes slide down until they focused on my hand, the right one, and then my finger. The one that had pulled the trigger. The finger that had ended Clayton Eugene Sartain's life. I twitched the lethal finger, watching the joints move, remembering the feel of that cold metal trigger against my skin.

What was I doing at Clay's funeral? I ought to be in the detention center. Locked up. Put away for the rest of my life.

The funeral-home men lowered Clay's casket into the ground. Dad let me toss the first handful of dirt into Clay's grave. Then we stayed behind as everyone else left the cemetery—a quiet line of people in their Sunday clothes, walking back through the woods to their cars parked along Mouse Creek Road.

"Why didn't the funeral-home men cover up the casket before they left?" I asked, staring at the mounds of dark earth piled neatly beside the grave.

Mom and Dad looked at each other like neither one wanted to answer. Finally, Dad said, "They'll come back later."

"When we're not here," Mom added.

I nodded, imagining all that dirt crashing down on top of Clay's casket. I didn't know what Mom and Dad were thinking, but my mind was choking with Clay thoughts. I wasn't ever going to see him again. His laugh was gone. His jokes. His voice. The way he draped his arm across my shoulder and gave me this sideways hug when we walked in the woods. All gone. Killed. Killed with my .410.

"Let's go back to the house and eat some of that food," Dad said in a shaky voice. He started walking toward the road like he was going to go eat lunch whether we followed him or not.

Mom looked at me. "Daniel needs more time here," she said.

Dad walked a few more steps, then stopped. He turned and stared back at the grave. Shaking his head, he reached into his coat pocket and found his pack of cigarettes. He shook one out and lit up.

"Can't stay here one second longer," he said, blue-gray smoke curling into the air. "Good thing I brought my truck."

"We'll catch up with you at the house," Mom said.

When Dad was gone, Mom pulled me close. "We'll stay as long as you want," she whispered into my hair. "Clay would like that."

Part of me wanted to stay there forever, my arms wrapped around Mom's soft, cushy waist, feeling her arms squeezing me tight. Like I was her baby again and she wasn't going to let anything bad happen to me.

The other part wanted to run away, screaming and yelling—telling everybody in the world that Clay's dying was all my fault. My fault. The preacher's eyes had said it all. I was always going to be that boy who killed his uncle.

How could I ever get past that? How could I live with it? I wanted to ask Mom those questions, but I couldn't get the words out. They were buried inside me, like my trembling body was a coffin and those words, those horrible questions, would rot inside me forever.

My stomach lurched as I broke away from Mom and took off running, stumbling in my uncomfortable shoes. I didn't know where I was going, but I knew I didn't want to be here anymore. Not with Clay in that box.

I didn't want to go home, either. Our tiny house would be crammed with people trying to make us feel better with food and hugs. Trying to comfort us with words like they had when Grandmama and Granddaddy died.

"Daniel, please come back," Mom called.

I heard her running after me and I was afraid she'd fall in her high-heeled shoes. But I couldn't make myself slow down.

"You don't have to eat or do anything you don't want to do—I promise," Mom said. "You're going to get past this terrible thing that happened. I reckon it'll take a very long time . . . but you'll heal. I know you will."

I couldn't imagine healing as I ran on through the woods with Mom behind me, trying to catch up. This wasn't like breaking my wrist when I was eight. Dr. Harris had put a cast on that to help me heal. A big white plaster cast that all the kids at school signed with Magic Markers.

No one could make a cast big enough to heal the hurt I felt now, I thought as my shoe hit a tree root hidden in the pine straw.

I felt myself going down, hurtling through the pine-scented air, falling face-first into the brown straw. For a moment, I just lay there, feeling my heart gallop beneath my suit coat, feeling the aches in my knees where they hit the ground and the sting of pine straw against my hot cheeks. And that hollow feeling inside from getting the breath knocked out of me.

Mom got there before I could pull myself up. She covered me with her body, kissing the back of my head, cradling me in her arms, murmuring how much she loved me. As she helped me up and walked me back to the car, I felt her trying to heal me.

chaptertwelve

The only thing that kept me going that afternoon when Mom and I got back to the house was Clay's voice in my head.

"What'd you think of Bill and Stanley from Wal-Mart?" Clay whispered as I sat at the kitchen table, surrounded by a houseful of chattering people, wishing I could disappear. I felt like a glass boy with everyone talking over me, around me, behind my back. Like if they talked directly to me I might shatter. And they'd have a mess to clean up.

"Looked like they were about to bust out crying. Never would have guessed they liked me that much." Clay laughed his high-pitched laugh, making my ears ring.

I felt the corners of my mouth twitch, then turn up slightly as I pinched off a bite of fried chicken and stuffed it into my mouth. Chewing it slow. Mashing it real good with my teeth. Feeling its grease on the roof of my mouth.

It tasted better than I thought it would. I ate another bite and glanced around at Mom and Dad and all the neighbors crowded into our tiny house.

Could they hear Clay? Of course not. I could tell by the way they kept right on talking and wolfing down sweet potato pie and chicken rice casserole like we were celebrating something joyful instead of mourning for someone dead.

Clay's voice was just for me now. Inside my head. Keeping me going when I didn't feel like I should even be in the world, I hurt so much.

"Did you try the potato salad?" Mom appeared, holding out a Tupperware bowl full of something lumpy and yellow.

I shook my head. "Thanks, Mom, but I can't hold anything else," I said, pretending I'd stuffed myself, even though I'd only managed to eat two bites of chicken and a couple of potato chips. The chips had crunched inside my head, making it hurt.

"You've hardly eaten a bite," Mom said, looking at me like her eyes could see all the way to the pit of my empty stomach.

"Hey, Daniel, wanna go outside?" My friend Eric appeared next to Mom, motioning for me to follow him and his twin sister, Nicole.

I looked at Mom, thinking she'd say no; I wanted to go. It felt like a year since I'd talked to the twins, though it had only been a week.

"Go hang out with your friends," Mom said, grabbing my plate. "I'll stash this in the refrigerator for later."

Nobody seemed to notice as the twins and I weaved our way through the living room full of adults. I closed the heavy front door behind us, shutting off all the sounds of grown-up conversation.

Even though they were twins, Eric and Nicole didn't look alike at all. Eric had big bones, a giant round head, and a really huge nose. He was blond and blue-eyed and he always had this sneaky expression on his face, like he was up to something.

Nicole was tiny for her age and real cute, though I'd never want anyone else to know I thought that about her. I liked the way her dark brown bangs fell down all messy in her eyes. And how her breath always smelled like mints. Clay said I ought to ask her to be my girlfriend. But I thought I was too young for that sort of stuff.

"It's chilly out here," Nicole said, backing into the porch swing and tucking the edges of her black skirt under her legs. Eric and I sat in metal chairs with white paint flaking off. We looked at each other until Eric's right eye started twitching. He rubbed his eye, making it all red, then cleared his throat.

"We wanted to come over here a couple of days ago. Mom wouldn't let us. She said you probably didn't want any company," Eric said.

"I wouldn't have minded," I said, glancing down at my black leather church shoes. My feet throbbed with pain. I bent down and started to untie a shoelace, then stopped. So my feet hurt. I deserved to suffer.

"We missed you at school this week," Nicole said. She tossed her hair back on her forehead, then grinned, showing braces with pink rubber bands.

"Yeah, I'm tired of looking at your empty desk," Eric

said. "When you coming back, Dan? Mrs. Pettibone said it might be Monday."

"Don't know." I squashed a moth with my hurting shoe, grinding it into the porch floor until it was a greasy gray spot. I wanted to tell the twins I was never coming back.

But I knew sooner or later I'd have to go to school. And walk into my fifth-grade classroom. In front of all those faces staring at me. Every kid in my room would be thinking about me shooting my uncle. If today were that day, I would surely break into a million pieces.

"Come back Monday," Nicole said. "You can't stay home forever."

"I'll think about it," I said, watching a chipmunk poke its head into the dark hole of a drainage pipe in our front yard.

After that, it was like the twins ran out of things to say to me. Nicole hummed a song we'd been practicing at school as she made the porch swing squeak louder and louder. Eric picked invisible stuff off the sleeve of his gray suit coat.

"You say something, D-Man," Clay's voice whispered in my head. *"They came here to offer their sympathy, and all you can do is sit there and stare at 'em? Open your mouth and speak. What do you think your voice is for?"*

I shook my head, then stared across the front-yard grass at a green Ford pickup chugging its way toward town.

Granddaddy had a truck like that. I could barely remember that old truck—or Granddaddy. Even though I remembered us fishing, his face seemed fuzzy when I tried to imagine how he looked. I wondered how long it would take for Clay's face to get all blurry in my mind.

"You okay?" Eric stopped picking at his coat sleeve and gave me a puzzled look. "It's like you went somewhere—like you're not on the porch with us."

I didn't feel okay. I used to feel good around Eric and Nicole—comfortable, like they were my own brother and sister. But today I felt like I hardly knew them. Like I was somebody totally different since the accident. And they were strangers.

I had changed so much in just one week. And I was still changing, like a superhero going backwards. Losing my special powers. Shriveling into a heap of gooey gunk on the floor, like that moth. Then rising up out of the stinking mess, a full-blown monster like Dad. Howling and flinging my fists, hating the whole world.

"We can go in, if you're not feeling good," Eric said. "It's kinda cold to be sitting on the porch anyway."

"Mom brought lemon meringue pie," Nicole said. "Let's get a slice before it's all gone."

"No." I shook my head. "I'm not hungry."

"That's one for the record books," Eric said.

Nicole stopped swinging, skidding her feet against the porch floor. She slid off the swing and walked over to me and put her tiny, soft hand on my hand, covering my fingers—even the one that had pulled the trigger.

"You're going to be okay, Daniel," she said. "It wasn't your fault, what happened to Clay."

"Nicole?" Eric gave his sister a warning look. "You know Mom said we shouldn't say anything about . . . you know . . . the accident."

I winced when Eric said "the accident." I'd heard the

accident word over and over since Clay went down in the woods. But that word sounded different when Eric said it. It hurt even more.

Accident was the same as *tragedy*, one of our vocabulary words from a few weeks ago. Mrs. Pettibone had explained that like most words, *tragedy* had several different meanings. It could be a type of drama or play.

Now, after what had happened to Clay, I'd learned one of the other meanings of the *tragedy* word. The meaning I'd memorized for the vocabulary test but not really thought much about until now. Tragedy: A disastrous event, especially one involving distressing injury or loss of life. I knew all about tragedy now. And disaster. And distressing injury or loss of life.

It didn't matter whether or not Nicole or Eric or anyone else in the world stopped themselves from talking about the accident when they were around me. I knew what they were thinking. I could feel their thoughts in the air. Could smell their thoughts of tragedy and distressing injury or loss of life as strong as if they were fried chicken.

• • •

"You are pathetic, D-Man," Clay told me in my room that night. *"Stretched out on your bed. Frowning. Holding your stomach."*

"It hurts."

"Of course it hurts. Those are hunger pangs you're feeling. You didn't eat enough of Della Hooper's fried chicken to keep a bird going."

"Birds don't eat fried chicken."

"*Is that so?*"

"You know it's so. You know everything about birds. And rabbits. And guns."

After everybody left, I'd searched the garage for my .410, but I didn't find it. Dad had moved it to another hiding place. That was my gun Dad was hiding. Clay had given it to me for my eleventh birthday. And I wanted it back.

chapterthirteen

Clay's voice woke me better than any alarm clock Monday morning. He didn't ring or buzz or play music. But his voice in my head was loud when he said, *"Get up, D-Man. Put on your clothes. You're going back to school today."*

"Yeah, right." I groaned, rolling over. The thought of walking into that redbrick building full of kids and teachers made my stomach churn.

Anyway, I couldn't go back to school until I found my gun. I'd decided to throw it in the lake. Like I should have done that day in the woods with Clay. It wouldn't change what had happened, but maybe I'd feel better knowing it was buried in the muddy lake bottom.

"Stop thinking about that gun, D-Man." Clay's voice in my head sounded alarmed. *"Get up. Put on your clothes. You'll be late for school if you don't hurry."*

I couldn't ignore Clay's voice, so I did everything he

said, like a boy on autopilot. A robotic boy dressing, guzzling down milk, chewing mouthfuls of frozen waffle without thinking or tasting or feeling much of anything.

Mom's week off from work had ended Sunday night. Her shift had started at midnight. She wouldn't get home until I was already at school. Dad's snores coming from his bedroom told me he was still asleep. I wouldn't have to see his face or talk to him before I left the house.

A horn honked in the driveway. Mrs. Pettibone was already here. I grabbed my backpack, unlocked the door, and rushed outside, feeling cold air chap my face.

I almost stumbled down the porch steps when I saw Mrs. Hardy waving from the window of a cherry red Mustang convertible. I guessed it was probably a 1970 model.

"Wasn't Mrs. Pettibone supposed to pick me up?" I asked, sliding into the black vinyl bucket seat next to the counselor. The black dashboard was cracked near the steering wheel, but everything else looked good for an old car.

"You disappointed?" Mrs. Hardy asked, looking me over with her inquiring eyes.

"No." I pulled the seat belt across my lap. The heavy metal clasp made a clicking sound as I buckled it.

"Good," Mrs. Hardy said, gunning the engine. She shifted gears and eased the car down the driveway, then stopped.

"It's really cold this morning. Where's your coat, Daniel?" Mrs. Hardy let the Mustang idle as she looked at me, waiting for my answer.

I shrugged. "In the hall closet, I guess."

"We've got time. Run back and find it. We don't want

you getting sick because you didn't wear your warm coat, do we?"

I shook my head and got out of the car.

The front door had locked behind me. I found the key in my pocket, twisted it in the lock, and slipped inside. Dad's snores coming from the bedroom told me he was still asleep.

The warm house air felt good as I walked toward the coat closet. Seeing my own pale face reflected in the hall mirror made me stop for a moment. The sadness in my eyes surprised me. I knew I felt sad inside. But I hadn't realized everyone could see my pain.

Was I ready to face the kids in my class? Maybe I should ask Mrs. Hardy to go on to school without me. Eleven-year-old boys weren't supposed to cry. *Ever.* At school, I'd have to pretend I was okay. And work really hard to keep the water-works from turning on. I didn't know if I could do that.

I opened the closet door and wrinkled my nose at the musty old clothes smell. My jacket hung in the middle of the row of coats and sweaters. It was the warm one with the down lining.

As soon as my fingers touched the soft cloth, I remembered. The last time I had worn this jacket, I was with Clay. Out in the woods. Rabbit hunting. How did it get back in the closet? Mom must have pulled it off me the day of the accident and hung it here.

Was it bloody?

My fingers recoiled like I'd just touched something wet. I didn't see any blood, but I couldn't look at the jacket without thinking about Clay and what had happened to him. Couldn't look at it without seeing blood that wasn't there staining the tan cloth with a color so deep it would never wash out.

I'd worn this same jacket when Clay took me to the county fair in Athens a few weeks ago. I remembered merry-go-round music playing as we walked through the sawdust-covered fairgrounds, eating cotton candy.

The bumper cars were my favorite ride that day. It didn't matter that Clay crashed his flaming orange car into my lime green one time after time.

"Drive that thing like you mean business or you'll never get anywhere!" Clay yelled, steering his car around and around, daring me to rear-end him.

Sparks sizzled across the metal floor as I stomped the gas pedal all the way down and chased my uncle.

Thinking about that now creeped me out. Clay wouldn't be taking me to the fair next year. We'd never have fun like that again.

I shoved my jacket all the way to the back of the rack, pushing the weight of the other clothes against it. Hard. Like it was a bumper car and I was totaling it out. Digging deeper, I found a lighter coat and pulled it on.

On my way back to the door, I stopped in front of the hallway mirror. The light jacket felt tight on my shoulders. The sleeves were short. But I wasn't changing it. No way.

"You were in there a long time," Mrs. Hardy said when I got back in the Mustang. "Is that your warmest coat?"

"Yeah," I said, hooking my seat belt, clenching my teeth at the clicking sound of the buckle.

"Must be made from some really warm but deceptively lightweight material."

"It's warm enough," I said, leaning my face against the cold window glass.

Mrs. Hardy steered the car down our driveway and turned onto Mouse Creek Road. Six-cylinder, I thought, listening to the little chugging sounds the engine made as the Mustang motored up the road toward town.

"I'm glad you're coming back to school today, Daniel," Mrs. Hardy said without taking her sharp eyes off the road. "I know it's hard, but it's the best thing for you to do."

I could tell she was a good driver by the smooth way she shifted gears. But this cool Mustang didn't feel like an old-lady car.

"This your car, Mrs. Hardy?"

"What do you think?"

I shrugged. "Doesn't seem like the kind of car somebody like you would drive."

"So, what kind of car should a decrepit thirty-eight-year-old woman like me drive, Daniel?"

"I don't know. Volkswagen? Toyota?"

Mrs. Hardy laughed, making dimples crease her cheeks. "My Corolla's in the shop today. Anyway, I thought you'd enjoy a ride in my Mustang."

"You have two cars?"

"This 1970 Mustang was my high school graduation gift from my parents. I'm too sentimental to get rid of it."

"I'd keep it forever. Do you let down the top?"

"Every once in a while. I only drive my 'Stang on special occasions. You coming back to school today certainly qualifies. How do you feel about coming back?" Mrs. Hardy glanced at me, then turned her eyes back to the road.

"I thought we were talking about your car," I said, listening to the flapping sounds of the convertible top overhead. The old car smelled like a mildewed tent.

"We were." Mrs. Hardy looked at me again. "And we can stick to car talk if that's what you want, Daniel. But I'd really like to know how you're feeling about school this morning."

I let out a sigh. "Guess I'm okay with it," I answered, even though okay was a long way from how I felt.

Mrs. Hardy glanced at me, then turned her eyes back to the road. "It's okay, you know, not wanting to come back to school today. I would understand if you felt that way."

I nodded. For a moment, I considered telling Mrs. Hardy exactly how I felt.

How I dreaded walking into my classroom. How I'd rather be at home, in my bed, with the quilt pulled over my face. How I wanted to find my .410 and throw it in the lake so I wouldn't feel so guilty.

How for the past few days I'd even thought I might want to point that gun at myself and take my shot.

She wanted to know. But I couldn't make those words come out.

"Mrs. Pettibone tells me they've missed you most in reading group. I hear you're one of the best readers in fifth grade. Your teacher brags on you all the time at lunch."

"Reading is my favorite subject." I pressed my face against the window glass, trying not to think about all the times Clay and I had read comic books together. I wondered if my teacher would make me read out loud in reading group today. I didn't think I could do that.

We were coming up on the only stoplight in Newton-ville. It hung over the middle of a four-way intersection near the Quick Pantry where Dad bought his cigarettes. The light turned red. Mrs. Hardy downshifted and eased the Mustang to a stop. I felt motor vibrations through the cold vinyl seat as we waited for the light to change.

Mrs. Hardy looked over at me. "Let's chat in my office a few minutes before you go to your classroom. Maybe that will help."

I nodded. "I'm a little nervous."

"That's to be expected," Mrs. Hardy said as the light changed to green.

Mrs. Hardy turned on Main Street. I watched the famil-iar houses pass by—huge white Victorians with towers and silvery tin rooftops. We passed the Baptist church, a long, low wooden building with a barnlike recreation center be-side it, and the old train depot on the town square.

City Hall stood next to the depot, a cream brick build-ing with four white columns. Across from that, the town fountain bubbled water. A wooden swing hung from one of the low branches of a tree near the fountain. As we passed by, I looked at the swing, moving in the breeze, and thought about Clay and me sitting there together.

Had it only been two weeks since we'd come to the square in his pickup, "just to see what's happening in town," as he always said? Nothing ever happened in our town . . . until the accident. Nothing good would ever happen again with Clay gone.

I sighed and turned in my seat, watching the swing and fountain fade out of sight. Mrs. Hardy glanced at me with a concerned look in her eyes, then turned back to the road.

When we got to school, Mrs. Hardy steered the Mustang up the long drive to the teachers' parking lot. She pulled into a narrow space between a green Volkswagen and a white Toyota.

We walked into the building together, me with my black backpack and Mrs. Hardy lugging her briefcase. I tried not to look into the school secretary's eyes as Mrs. Hardy motioned me past the teachers' lounge and down a hallway to her office door.

chapterfourteen

The walls of Mrs. Hardy's office were turquoise. At first I didn't like the color. But the more I looked at it, the more it pulled me in, until I felt like I was standing in a big aquarium.

On the wall behind her desk hung a giant picture of a kid walking hand in hand with a woman who looked like his mom. In one corner, there was a kid-sized octagonal table and eight blue plastic chairs.

A futon with a wrinkled tan cover was next to the table. A bright yellow flower made from clay jutted from the wall over the futon. I could tell it was clay because the paint didn't go all the way to the edges, leaving the rough orange clay exposed.

I walked over to the wall behind the table and studied a poster called "The Chart of Faces." The heading was "Stages of Grief," and each face had a different expression. The last face smiled at me.

"Daniel, pull one of those chairs over here to my desk, so we can see each other while we talk."

I did what Mrs. Hardy said, gritting my teeth at the scraping sounds the chair made as I dragged it across the floor. I sat down, feeling like I was a little too big for the seat. Mrs. Hardy didn't seem to notice.

"First, I want you to know something," she said. "You can come to my office anytime you want. Do you know how to make the time-out signal?"

"The time-out sign from ball games?"

Mrs. Hardy nodded.

"Sure." I pointed my right-hand fingers into my left hand, forming the giant time-out *T*.

"Good. Whenever you need to come to my office, just make that signal for Mrs. Pettibone. Then get up and walk down the hall and come on in here.

"And you don't have to talk at all while you're here, Daniel. You can read or draw at the table or just sit here and take a deep breath. My office is a safe place."

I nodded, wondering if I could spend the whole day in the counselor's office.

"We'll be talking some on your regular visits. Is there anything you want to talk about now? Before you go to your classroom?"

"Nope," I said.

"Your mom asked me to tell you something this morning. She wanted you to know that she and your dad are going to a counselor in Athens."

I studied the big clay flower over the futon. Why hadn't

somebody painted that flower all the way to the edges so all that raw clay wouldn't show? And why hadn't Mom told me herself about counseling? I wanted to ask Mrs. Hardy those questions, but I couldn't.

"Your parents have some issues to work out," Mrs. Hardy said. "Hopefully their counseling sessions will help. And your dad is getting some additional counseling, to help him deal with his own issues—especially his alcohol problem."

I couldn't imagine my parents going to a counselor. But I couldn't imagine me sitting in a counselor's office, either. And here I was.

When Mrs. Hardy was done talking to me, she opened the office door and we walked down the hall together. As we passed by the classrooms lining the hallway, I heard familiar school sounds. Voices reading aloud. A piano playing "Jingle Bell Rock." The notes sounded out of tune to me.

"Can anybody tell me the capital of Georgia?" A teacher's voice asked as we passed the third-grade room.

"Everybody knows it's Atlanta," a girl's bossy voice answered.

"I talked to your classmates last Friday, Daniel. They're so excited you're coming back this morning," Mrs. Hardy said as we got closer to my fifth-grade classroom.

I nodded and made my face smile at the counselor even though I felt like crying. I hadn't even walked into my classroom yet and already I knew coming back to school was a big mistake.

"Well, here we are," Mrs. Hardy said, stopping by the

open door of my room. "Remember what I told you—about the time-out signal. Mrs. Pettibone will understand."

"Okay," I said. I took a deep breath, then looked into the classroom.

Mrs. Pettibone was writing something on the board. I stared at the twenty-six kids sitting at desks, writing their assignments on notebook paper, and felt jittery inside.

I knew every one of those faces. Knew each kid's name. I'd been all the way through school with most of them. But today, I felt like I was walking into a roomful of strangers as I forced myself to step inside.

I felt everyone staring at me as I waited for Mrs. Pettibone to finish writing on the board. I tried to make my face smile, but my mouth wouldn't move.

When Mrs. Pettibone turned and saw me, she smiled. "Daniel. How wonderful to have you back."

"Thanks, Mrs. Pettibone." I heard Mrs. Hardy's shoe heels tapping against the hall floor as she left. I wanted to make the time-out signal and run after her. Instead, I walked to my desk near the middle of the third row, trying not to hear the words *uncle killer* humming in the air. Nobody was really saying those words, but I knew every kid in the room was thinking about what had happened in the woods.

"*Psssst* . . . welcome back," Nicole whispered from her desk across the aisle. She puffed her bangs out of her face and leaned closer. "You want to come over to our house after school? We've got that Batman movie you wanted to see. Of course Mom will make us do our homework first."

"Some other day?" I tried to smile at Nicole. "I'm still . . . well, you know."

Nicole looked disappointed, but she nodded like she understood.

As I glanced back toward the front of the room, I caught Travis Jones giving me a look. He turned his face away as soon as he saw that I had noticed. Travis was always trouble. He had beaten me up on the first day of kindergarten, and every school year he got even meaner.

"Class, I promised you a social studies test today," Mrs. Pettibone said, causing everyone but me to groan. I just sat there wondering how I was going to take a test this morning. A test full of questions I knew nothing about.

"And I must keep my promises, right?" the teacher said, handing stacks of test papers to each front-row kid to pass out.

While the tests circulated around the room, Mrs. Pettibone walked over to my desk. "Did Mrs. Hardy tell you about the signal?"

I nodded.

"You don't need my permission to leave the room. Just make the signal and I'll know where you're going. And don't worry about how you do on this test today, Daniel. We'll call it practice. You can take a makeup after you've had a chance to read the book and go over the material." The teacher looked at me with kind eyes over the rims of her glasses as she handed me a test paper.

I nodded and glanced down. None of the questions made sense. The words looked like a foreign language.

"Think of this as a warm-up," Mrs. Pettibone said, patting my arm.

I had always liked for my teacher to pat my arm. But

today I didn't want her to touch me. The teacher's hand on my skin felt heavy, like I could feel it all the way through to my bones. I didn't want to feel that much right now. I just wanted everyone to leave me alone.

Mrs. Pettibone walked back to her desk and settled into her chair. I saw her looking at me with a concerned expression and I wanted to make the time-out signal. But I didn't.

All around me, kids penciled in their answers. A boy in the back row coughed. The big round clock over the board made humming sounds as the hands moved forward.

I usually got As on social studies tests. But today, as I tried to read the first question, the words jumbled together.

This was so hopeless. I slapped my hand down hard on the test paper, then did it again and again. The loud whomping noises made everybody stop filling in answers. They all turned their eyes on me, looking like they expected me to do something really crazy.

I felt my face flush as the words *uncle killer* hummed in my head again. The sounds were louder this time. I tried to hold myself still in my desk, tried to control the shaking. But it was no use. I thought I saw blood, too, on the finger that had pulled the trigger. I jerked the test paper over my hand, trying to hide all that red.

Uncle killer, uncle killer, uncle killer. The words wouldn't stop. I pressed my hands over my ears and squeezed my eyes shut, trying to blot everything out. "Stop it. *Stop it!*"

"What's wrong, Daniel?" Mrs. Pettibone was at my desk when I looked up, staring at me with creases wrinkling her forehead. She reached down to pat my arm. I jerked it away.

I wanted to yell, "Don't touch me!" Instead, I jammed

my fingers into the palm of my other hand, making the T-shaped signal.

Mrs. Pettibone nodded as I slid out of my desk and walked through the classroom door, breaking into a sprint when I got to the hall. It only took me a few seconds to reach Mrs. Hardy's office.

I knocked.

"Come in," Mrs. Hardy's voice answered.

My hand shook as I opened the door and stumbled into the turquoise room. I felt the color, deep and calm, swirling all around me. "Make yourself at home, Daniel," Mrs. Hardy said. Then she turned back to her desk, like she was giving me some privacy. This was a time-out, like I was in a really tough ball game and I needed a few minutes to decide what to do next.

I watched the counselor's fingers dance across the computer keyboard, making tiny clicking sounds as words appeared, flickering across the gray screen, and I felt myself getting calmer.

Mrs. Hardy had said I could make the signal at my teacher and come here anytime and I didn't have to talk.

So I walked over to the futon and lay down, pressing my face against the soft velvety material, pulling my legs up and hugging myself into a ball. I was a roly-poly bug, all closed up to the world. I didn't want to be at school or at home or anywhere. I felt so sad I didn't know if I wanted to be at all.

Mrs. Hardy's fingers kept tapping on the keyboard while I tried to wipe my whole brain clean. Like my brain was a computer that had nothing but errors.

A computer could be fixed. But I didn't know about me. Maybe I was doomed.

Like the actor who had played Superman in those old black-and-white TV shows Clay and I used to watch. George Reeves was his name. Clay said he jumped out of a window one day and he couldn't fly.

But I knew better. I'd read a story about him in the newspaper. That Superman had shot himself with a gun. I wondered if I could do something like that. And the thought scared me.

"Daniel, is there anything I can do to help you?" I didn't have to look. I could feel Mrs. Hardy's inquiring eyes taking me in, analyzing me like I was an error on her computer screen.

I hugged myself tighter. "You said I didn't have to talk. I could come here anytime and you wouldn't make me say a word."

Mrs. Hardy got up and walked over to the futon. I felt the cushion shift as she sat down. She put her warm hand on my back and patted me, like I was her own son.

I flinched and hugged myself even tighter.

"I did say that, Daniel. But I didn't promise not to talk to you."

"What?" I sat up, blinking my eyes at the counselor. This wasn't fair. Maybe I wouldn't have come in here if I'd known she was going to talk to me. It was a grown-up trick.

"I have an idea," Mrs. Hardy said, going back to her desk and opening the top drawer. "Somebody told me you've got a real passion for comic books. Is that correct?"

I nodded.

"Just so happens I keep a few in my desk drawer—in case I get bored with this counseling work I do all day. Wanna see what I've got?"

Mrs. Hardy dared me with her face, wiggling her eyebrows and looking at the desk drawer, then back at me.

"Show me," I said.

chapterfifteen

Mrs. Hardy and I read comics together in her office every day during my regular counseling sessions. She liked Wonder Woman best. I was partial to the Invincible Iron Man.

"You read through my whole comic collection in two weeks," Mrs. Hardy said as I put away the comics we'd finished that morning. "Guess we'll have to find you some other reading material."

"I could bring my favorites from home. Bet you haven't read 'The Mystery of the Mild-Mannered Superman.'"

I'd been reading that same comic, the one Clay and I were reading together not long before the accident, in my room every night for over a week. The words didn't jumble when I read those pages. Still, I could never seem to finish. Not without Clay there.

"I have a better idea. What do you say we head down to

the school library? I bet the librarian has some great books on his shelves for an advanced reader like you."

Mr. Robbins, a skinny kidlike man with curly black hair, spent a long time going through the aisles of books, showing me which ones I might want to read. I decided to start with a classic, *The Adventures of Tom Sawyer*, because the librarian said it was his all-time favorite.

"Have you noticed anything different about your dad?" Mrs. Hardy asked as we walked back to her office, admiring the Christmas decorations.

"He doesn't drink as much," I said, stopping to stare at a crooked green construction-paper Christmas tree on the first-grade classroom door. The ornaments on that tree were pictures of each kid's face outlined in a reindeer shape. I remembered the first-grade teacher, Mrs. Jonas, tracing my hands and feet to make my reindeer outline when I was in that room.

I followed Mrs. Hardy on down the hall and into her office, closing the door behind us. "And I can tell he's trying not to explode—I mean lose his temper."

"I know what you mean," Mrs. Hardy said. "And that's an improvement, isn't it? How's your mom doing?"

I slid into a blue plastic chair and looked up at the flower with the raw clay edges. "She's good," I said. "She got a promotion at work—line supervisor. She's on the day shift now."

"Wonderful news," Mrs. Hardy said. "You must be excited about that. And with Christmas right around the corner, you're about to have two whole weeks off from school."

Mrs. Hardy pulled out her swivel desk chair and sat at

her computer, twisting the seat back and forth until she got it into just the right position. She touched the keyboard with her long, red-nailed fingers and the screen came to life, flickering with words. I figured some of those words were about me, but I'd never tried to read what she was typing. It didn't seem like a polite thing to do.

"So, Daniel. What's number one on your Christmas wish list?"

I turned my face away and looked at the yellow flower again, biting my lip and trying not to tremble. I couldn't think of a single thing I wanted other than Clay back.

And when I thought about Christmas break starting in less than a week, my eyes almost teared up. How was I going to get through each day without talking to Mrs. Hardy?

The counselor got up and walked over and picked a dead leaf off a fern in a purple pot on the windowsill. She turned back to me. "How about number two?"

I sighed, staring harder at the clay flower. I didn't have a number two.

"Let's change the subject. The boy who's been taunting you. What's his name?"

"Travis Jones."

"Is he bothering you now?"

I looked down at my book, *The Adventures of Tom Sawyer,* wondering how Mrs. Hardy knew about Travis. Flipping past the table of contents and the introduction, I read silently, "Chapter One. Tom Plays, Fights, and Hides."

"Is he?"

"Nope." I didn't want to tell Mrs. Hardy why Travis wasn't bothering me anymore. About how I had stopped him from calling me a coward by introducing him to my fist in the boys' bathroom last Wednesday.

"Mr. Owens said you hit Travis. In the nose. Did you?"

"What?" I looked up from my book to see Mrs. Hardy standing beside me, giving me her intense look. Her earrings dangled, long and turquoise, as she waited for my answer.

"Okay. I hit him . . . once," I said, turning my face back to the book, trying to read words that jumbled together.

"Hitting Travis might have felt good," Mrs. Hardy said. "But was it the right way to handle that situation?"

"I couldn't stop my fist from smashing into Travis's face. I know it was wrong, but . . ."

"You're lucky you didn't get in trouble with Mr. Owens," Mrs. Hardy said. "The principal is cutting you some slack, you know. Giving you a chance to straighten up. He asked me to talk to you about it."

"I took care of Travis and he's not bothering me anymore. He hit me in the restroom a couple of months ago and he didn't get in trouble."

"Did you tell anyone?"

"No. Can I read my book now? Mrs. Pettibone says I'm all caught up on my classwork. And you said you wanted me to read real books instead of comics. Can I just do that now?"

"You might be caught up, but your test scores are still down, Daniel. We'll have to work on that after the holidays."

"I'll pull my grades up after Christmas. I promise."

"I'm going to hold you to that promise," Mrs. Hardy said. She picked more dead leaves off the fern until it looked naked.

"I'm feeling good, really." I glanced down at my book and studied a picture of Tom Sawyer standing in front of a fence.

"Glad to hear that," Mrs. Hardy said. She walked back to her desk. Her swivel chair squeaked as she sat down.

I watched Mrs. Hardy type. The red hair on the back of her head stuck out, all wispy, like it needed combing down. I wondered what she'd think if I told her feeling good was just an act.

What if I told her how I practiced my *Daniel's okay* look every day in front of the bathroom mirror, like I was rehearsing for a play? Turning my lips up at the corners so it looked like I was smiling. Making these loud chuckling sounds so I'd be ready if someone told a joke.

I looked down at the book again. The words were still jumbled. I could get through Mrs. Hardy's comics. But no matter how hard I tried, I couldn't read a page of words like this.

Couldn't read a test question either and understand it. Couldn't sit through a whole TV show anymore or do my math homework or even brush my teeth without resting halfway through.

But I couldn't tell anyone about that. Mrs. Hardy and Mrs. Pettibone and Mom were working so hard to make me feel good again, I had to pretend I was okay, even if my grades were slipping . . . and I felt like hitting the whole world.

Mrs. Hardy turned in her chair and gave me a smile. "The book, Daniel. Read the book," she said.

I made my lips smile back at the counselor. Made my

eyes focus on the book page again. But instead of reading, I wanted to throw Tom Sawyer across the office. I didn't want to read about some prehistoric boy in plaid pants whitewashing a fence.

I wanted more comics. Comics didn't have so many words to jumble. They were quick reading, and to the point. I wanted to read the one about Superman's death. Clay had told me it'd be at the Comic Exchange store in December. Today was December fourteenth. It was probably already there.

"What's wrong, Daniel?"

Mrs. Hardy was looking at me like she was trying to read my thoughts. I wanted to tell her what I was thinking. I really did. But I didn't know where to begin.

I looked back down at the book and something on the white tabletop caught my eye. An orange bug with black spots.

"There's a bug on the table, Mrs. Hardy."

"You telling me my gorgeous turquoise office has roaches?" Mrs. Hardy laughed and turned back to her computer.

"If you think that bug is going to get you out of reading that wonderful book, think again," she said. "There's not much in this world that scares me. We won't be fleeing my office today because of a roach."

I looked closer at the tiny insect.

"It's a ladybug," I said, flicking at it with my finger. The bug flipped over, revealing miniature black legs wiggling and a dot-sized black face.

"Those ladybugs are always looking for a warm place in

the winter," Mrs. Hardy said. "They sneak in through cracks in the walls."

"Mom says ladybugs bring good luck."

"She's right. Let the bug crawl into your hand so you can set her free in the hallway and share the luck. And when you come back, how about reading aloud? I'd enjoy hearing *Tom Sawyer* in your voice," Mrs. Hardy said.

"Okay." I sighed, wondering how I could read all those jumbled words aloud. I'd have to give it a try.

"Oh, and when you set your ladybug free, you're supposed to say, 'Ladybug, ladybug, fly away home. Your house is on fire and your children are gone.'"

"Yeah, right." I looked down. Ladybug's legs were moving slower now, like the insect was battery-powered and the battery was running out of juice. I tapped at the bug and its legs speeded up again. Then they stopped.

I flipped the ladybug over. "Go on. I'm setting you free," I said, pushing at the tiny orange and black shell, trying to make the insect scoot across the tabletop. "Ladybug, ladybug, fly away home."

"Daniel, you listening to me? I said you could take your friend out in the hall."

"Okay." I tipped the bug over on its back again with my finger. The tiny black legs were still. Ladybug wasn't going anywhere. I blinked back something wet in my eye.

"Daniel?" Mrs. Hardy got up and walked over to the table. She pulled out one of the blue chairs and wedged her grown-up body into it. "I thought you were going to escort your ladybug out to the hall."

"I can't." I looked away at the chart of faces on the wall. I knew my mouth matched the face with the frown.

"Why not?"

"She's . . . dead."

Mrs. Hardy touched the ladybug with the tip of her finger. She sighed and reached over and put her hand on mine. "All living things die, Daniel. Even beautiful little orange and black ladybugs."

"Why?" I blurted the word like one of Dad's ugly curses as I looked up at Mrs. Hardy, jerking my hand away from hers. I didn't care about pretending anymore. I didn't have to feel good—or pretend I felt good—or be good if I didn't want to.

Mrs. Hardy's eyes got glassy-looking, like they were tearing up. "I can't answer your question, Daniel. Nobody really knows why we die. But we'll all die someday. You. Me. All the teachers. Every boy and girl in this school. And their parents and pets. Right down to the bugs hiding in the crevices of our homes and school building.

"Death happens and we can't do anything to change that. My husband died three years ago and I know I'll miss him until the day I die."

My eyes felt wet as I thought about Mom and Nicole and Eric and Mrs. Hardy dying. And Mrs. Pettibone and Mr. Hooper and Mrs. Hardy's husband and even Travis Jones . . . and Dad. Anger flared up inside me then, like a flame on Dad's cigarette lighter, burning my insides, making me feel hollow and charred.

"Why'd you say all those things to me, Mrs. Hardy? You're supposed to cheer me up—not make me feel worse."

"Is that what you think? I'm not a cheerleader, Daniel. I'm here to help you deal with the truth. You know, most people live a very long time—maybe into their seventies or eighties or even longer. They die slowly as their bodies age and eventually they wear out—sort of like an old car."

"Clay didn't get to wear out," I blurted.

"That's right. Sometimes a person dies suddenly, as your uncle did in that tragic accident. That's what it was, Daniel. An accident. Something that wasn't meant to happen. But it did happen and it wasn't your fault."

"It was my fault. I didn't shoot the rabbit like Clay wanted me to. I didn't let my finger pull the trigger. I was a chicken scaredy-cat. I got up and I let my gun fall across my chest. Let it point at Clay—"

"You didn't mean for that gun to fire."

"My finger was still on the trigger, Mrs. Hardy. And the cartridge was still loaded in the barrel. I didn't remember all those safety tips Clay told me the night before at his cabin. I got up with a loaded gun."

"Clay's death was an accident, Daniel. And that's the hardest kind of death to accept."

"I can't, Mrs. Hardy. I can't accept it." I couldn't help shouting those words at the counselor. And before I knew it, my fists pounded the tabletop. Pounded hard against the plastic surface until I felt my knuckles bruising. When I looked down, the ladybug was smashed.

"Look at me, Daniel," Mrs. Hardy said, guiding my face away from the flattened insect. "If Clay suffered at all, it wasn't for long. He probably didn't even realize what happened to him. Most likely, he didn't feel any pain. You'll eventually get past all the pain yourself. And you'll accept what happened to your uncle. You won't ever forget Clay, but as time goes on, you'll feel less sad."

I didn't see how that could be true. Clay wasn't ever coming back and I would always be the boy who shot his uncle. No matter how hard I tried, I was never going to pretend my way out of that.

chaptersixteen

"Hope you brought your permission slip," Nicole said as I followed the twins through drizzly rain to the bus loading zone. School was out for the Christmas holidays. Even though I didn't want to, Mom had talked me into going home with the twins.

"Got it right here," I said, climbing the bus steps. I pulled the note from my jeans pocket and handed it to the bus driver.

"What's this?" Mrs. Flanigan asked, squinting at the paper. Her gray-white hair was decorated with plastic poinsettias. She'd been our bus driver since second grade, but she still acted like she didn't know us.

"Permission slip," I said. "Mom says I can get off the bus today with Nicole and Eric Martin."

"Really?" Mrs. Flanigan looked up at me with a puzzled

expression. "This here note says 'Mrs. Hardy.' And that looks like her phone number to me."

"Oops." I stuffed Mrs. Hardy's note from our last session back into my pocket and fumbled around until I found the real slip.

"Okey-dokey, Mr. Daniel Sartain. You're good to go," the bus driver said, handing the note back to me.

"Two whole weeks of freedom, Dan," Eric said, punching at my shoulder as we slid into a seat. Nicole sat on the other side of me. I breathed in her peppermint smell.

"Can't you at least crack a smile or something?" Eric nudged my shoulder. "It's Christmas, Dan. You know, presents and days off from school and lots of candy—I mean, it's time to feel good."

"Quit picking on him, Eric," Nicole scolded.

The bus doors whooshed shut. I felt the huge yellow vehicle lunge forward as the driver put it into gear and followed the bus caravan down the drive to the road.

"I'm not picking on him," Eric said, reaching across me to bop his sister's arm.

"Will you cut it out?" I looked over at Eric and I wanted to punch his fat, round face. I felt my fist flexing between us on the bus seat as I turned away and made myself watch a fourth-grade girl in a seat across the aisle break off a giant chocolate Santa's head.

What was I thinking when I told the twins I'd go home with them this afternoon? We were barely away from school and already I knew it was a mistake.

All those happy holiday sounds around me on the bus

made it impossible not to think about Christmas. Last year, Clay gave me my Nintendo and we stayed up all night playing Super Mario Bros. He played football with me in the front yard the next day even though it was eighteen degrees outside.

"Hey, D-Man, go out long. I'm putting my arm into this one," Clay said, tossing me a high, spiraling pass.

I ran across the front-yard grass, muscles in my legs pumping, arms twisting, reaching upward, trying to snag the ball spinning toward me.

Smack! I felt rough tree bark bruise my skin as I crashed into a giant pine at the edge of the driveway. Then I felt Clay's hands, rubbing my scratched face, feeling to make sure my bones weren't broken.

"Man, you almost caught that thing," Clay said, pulling me up and helping me limp into the house.

Clay wouldn't be here on Christmas this year. I didn't want to be here. Didn't want to be around for a Christmas without Clay—or a life without him, either.

"Daniel, wake up. We're here," Nicole said, shaking my arm as the bus coasted to a stop outside the twins' yellow brick ranch house.

The first thing I saw when we walked into the twins' living room was an enormous Christmas tree. For a moment, I couldn't move or even catch my breath. But my eyes took it all in: shiny ornaments, glittery tinsel, the star tree topper the twins had made in first grade. I had a shiny silver star just like theirs somewhere in a box of Christmas tree decorations in our attic.

There were presents wrapped in red and green foil paper,

heaped beneath the tree. All that holiday cheer made me feel shaky inside.

"Like our tree?" Nicole asked, reaching behind it and plugging in the lights.

The tree exploded with multicolored twinkles. "It's nice," I said feeling my stomach gurgle as I watched colors glow in the green branches.

The wetness in my eyes caught me off guard. I turned away, staring at the red velvet sofa across the room, biting my lip, wishing Mom would pick me up. She was off work the whole week of Christmas. All I had to do was call and she'd be here in a minute. Our house was just down the next road.

I felt my fingers twitch as I glanced at the phone on the table by the sofa. I wanted to call Mom right now. Maybe I could come up with an excuse. I wasn't feeling good. That would do it.

"Mom's out doing some Christmas shopping, but we already got your present," Eric said, pressing a tiny red-foil envelope into my hand.

"But I . . . don't have anything for you and Nicole," I said, suddenly realizing that I hadn't gotten gifts for anyone this year.

"Don't worry about it," Eric said. "Who'd feel like shopping after . . . you know . . . what happened?"

"We don't need anything," Nicole said. "Open your gift."

My fingers barely cooperated as I struggled to tear the foil paper. Inside was a gift certificate for Comic Exchange. Now I could get "The Death of Superman."

"Come on, Dan. Let's go downstairs and play Ping-Pong. Seems like forever since we played a game," Eric said.

We clunked down the stairs to the basement recreation room, a dark-paneled cave full of every game and toy imaginable.

"Let's start a brand-new tournament." Eric grabbed a paddle from the table. He scooped up the tiny white ball and balanced it on the rubber-coated orange paddle top. He tapped the ball into the air, again and again, waiting for me to pick up my paddle.

Walking to the table seemed to take forever. My feet struggled to make each step. I'd probably played Ping-Pong with Eric and Nicole hundreds of times. But I didn't feel like playing today. Didn't feel like pretending. I didn't even feel like an eleven-year-old kid. I felt old. Too old for Ping-Pong games.

"What you waiting for? Let's play," Eric said when I finally got to the table.

Nicole pulled out a folding chair and positioned herself near the table so she could watch the game.

I looked at the second paddle on the table, studying the pattern on the orange plastic circle. I couldn't make my arm move. My muscles felt frozen, like I'd just stepped into a pocket of Arctic air.

"Go on, pick up that paddle and show Eric what you've got," Clay's voice in my head urged as I tried to extend my hand. *"You're the Ping-Pong champ, aren't you, D-Man?"*

"No," I said, letting my hand drop, slapping the table, making the paddle rattle. I beat the green table with my fist, hard. This was the hand that had pulled the trigger. How could it play Ping-Pong like nothing had happened?

"What's wrong, Daniel?" Nicole came over and put her

hand on my arm. I usually liked her peppermint breath and the touch of her hand. But for a moment, I thought I might be sick.

"Nothing," I said, pulling my arm away.

"You liked Ping-Pong before . . . you know . . . what happened," Eric said. He let the ball roll off his paddle and it clunk-clunk-clunked across the table, then rolled to the floor.

"I don't think I'm going to play anymore." That sick feeling welled up inside me again as I stared down at my shaking hands.

I couldn't play Ping-Pong. I couldn't give the twins a gift. Couldn't be happy like all the other kids. Christmas was too hard.

"I'll call your mom to come get you," Nicole said.

"Yeah, Dan. We'll play Ping-Pong when you're feeling better," Eric said.

We waited for Mom in the living room with the twins' Christmas tree twinkling all the colors of Christmas cheer. The longer I looked at the tree and the presents underneath it, the sadder I got.

• • •

"What happened this afternoon?" Mom asked in the car on the way home. "I thought spending time with your friends would cheer you up."

I looked over at Mom and tried to make my lips smile. But they wouldn't cooperate. I guess I was all out of pretend. "I just . . . you know, got to thinking about what

Christmas is going to be like without . . . Clay," I said in a weak voice.

Mom reached across the car seat and squeezed my arm.

"I reckon I know how you feel," she said. The car swerved a little off the road edge when she said that. But Mom got it back under control.

"We're all thinking about last Christmas and how much we miss Clay," Mom said. "He was such a big kid—he loved Christmas more than the rest of us put together."

chapterseventeen

Dad was waiting for us when we walked in the door, his fingers curled around a beer can. I tried to slip past him, but he caught my arm with his other hand.

"What's missin' from this living room?" Dad asked, gesturing all around with beer sloshing over the can rim.

I shrugged, smelling his beer breath, wishing he'd let go of my arm. His squeezing fingers hurt.

"Christmas treats," Mom said, getting a plate of gingerbread cookies from the kitchen and setting them on the coffee table.

Dad let go of my arm. He pointed his beer can toward the front windows. "How 'bout a Christmas tree? You see one, Daniel?"

We always moved the lamp table by Dad's recliner and put up our tree in front of the double windows. So people driving up Mouse Creek Road could see our lights.

"Well?" Dad took a long swig of beer. He crumpled the can and tossed it at the trash container in the kitchen. The can missed and thunked against the floor.

"You know there's no tree," I said, looking into Dad's bloodshot eyes, wishing he'd stop drinking. Wishing he'd stop pretending he had holiday spirit. We couldn't celebrate Christmas with Clay gone. It didn't seem right. Nothing seemed right anymore.

"Put on your warm coat, son. We're gonna cut us a tree," Dad said.

"You go on without me," I said. I didn't want a Christmas tree in our house. Clay was gone. He wouldn't be eating oyster stew with us on Christmas Eve. Or knocking on our door on Christmas morning, his arms full of gifts. Or acting like a great big kid when he took forever to open his presents.

Clay wouldn't be ringing in the new year with us, either. All because of me. I was never going to get over what I'd done to Clay. Never.

"Ain't going without you, son." Dad found his heavy parka in the hall closet and pulled it on. "It's gonna be chilly in them woods," he said, sorting through the coats and sweaters in the closet until he found my heavy jacket. He pulled the coat off its hanger and shoved the thing into my hands.

I started to shove my jacket back at Dad. Then I stopped. I didn't see any blood on the jacket, but I knew it was there. And I deserved to wear it. So I pulled it on over the lighter coat, not caring how tight it was or how many imaginary stains it had.

"Good boy. Now all we need is the bow saw and we can head to the woods," Dad said.

"Maybe Daniel doesn't want to go to the woods with you, Ray," Mom said. "Why don't the two of you go cut a tree at Gibbses' Christmas tree farm? That'd be a lot easier."

Dad paused by the door, looking at Mom, trying to make his thin lips smile. "We got our own trees growing in the woods. No reason to pay for one."

"It's okay, Mom," I said as Dad and I walked out to the porch. I deserve to go back to the woods, I thought, following Dad to the garage.

Cupping my hands against my face, I tried to stop shivering as I walked across the yard behind Dad. It had been raining. Everywhere I looked, trees and bushes and grass glistened with tiny beads of water, like the whole outdoors was decorated for Christmas.

"Wait here. I'll get the bow saw," Dad said, pulling open the garage door and disappearing inside the creaky wooden building.

I listened to Dad bumping around in there and thought about him hiding my .410 the day the game warden brought it back. The gun was gone when I searched the next day. Since then, I'd looked everywhere for that shotgun but still hadn't found it.

"Here you go," Dad said, coming out of the garage and handing me the rusty saw. For a moment, I thought my eyes might tear up. Usually, Clay used this saw. And we walked to the woods together and found a tree. We wouldn't do that again. Ever.

"Come on, Daniel," Dad said, heading down our driveway. "Gonna get dark on us if we don't hurry up."

I heard honking sounds as a giant V of Canadian geese flew toward the darkening horizon over Sartain Woods. I watched the birds a moment, then followed Dad across the meadow, holding the old saw away from my side so the jagged metal teeth wouldn't cut me.

Or maybe I should let the saw cut me, I thought as I remembered walking to the woods with Clay last month.

I tried to put that walk out of my mind as I followed Dad into the woods. He was a couple of inches shorter than his brother and his hair was darker. And he didn't walk long-legged. He limped.

But some things about Dad reminded me of Clay. They both had big ears. Mom called them generous. And broad shoulders. And they swung their arms the same when they walked.

Dad stopped for a minute, waiting for me to catch up. He spat on the ground, coughed, and wiped his mouth on the back of his glove. He got jittery then, twitching his fingers and staring over into the trees. I knew he was thinking about a cigarette.

"That counselor I been going to in Athens—he said I oughta quit smoking. I'm down to half a pack a day. Ain't that great, son?"

Dad didn't wait for my answer. He turned and started walking again, limping and weaving on the path, snapping the ends off low-hanging tree limbs as he made his way through the woods.

I should have said "Congratulations." That was the polite

thing to do. But I couldn't make the word come out of my mouth. Dad shouldn't have been smoking in the first place. Or drinking. Or making me walk in these cold woods to cut a Christmas tree. Clay and I always cut the tree. Dad was trying to take his place. And that wasn't right.

Dad would never be Clay.

We walked in silence for a while. At the lake, I stopped and watched geese float on the bluish green water. A great blue heron stood in shallow water near the shore, watching for fish.

I looked over to say something to Dad. But he was already way up the path. I ran after him, figuring he wouldn't stop at our ancestors' cabin, either. But when I got there, he was standing very still by the crumbling chimney, watching a white-tailed deer bolt through the trees.

"Too bad I didn't bring my hunting rifle. Been thinking 'bout taking up the sport again," Dad said.

As soon as the words left his mouth, Dad looked at me real quick. I could see that he was waiting for my reaction. Like I was going to say, "Yeah, Dad. Let's go deer hunting sometime."

Then another thought popped into my head. Dad wasn't thinking about *us* going deer hunting. Who'd want to go hunting with the boy who shot his uncle?

I glanced down at the bow saw in my hand, at the jagged metal teeth, wishing we'd just find a cedar and get this Christmas tree cutting over with.

"Guess I shouldn't have mentioned hunting," Dad said. "Come on, let's go find a tree. I smell one, right up there. You smell that cedar?"

Dad started walking, then stopped and looked back at me. "Know what these woods need, son? Houses. Lots of houses. Can't you see 'em already? All over these woods and around the lake? Lake lots go for big bucks."

I looked around, trying to imagine the neighborhood Dad was talking about. I couldn't see it. All I could see—all I wanted to see—was trees.

I'd learned to love these woods just as much as Clay, almost as much as I loved my uncle. We couldn't let anyone cut these trees. They were alive. And Clay loved them . . . right up till . . . he couldn't anymore. That was all my fault. I took the woods from Clay. I took everything.

"We'll have us a new house, too, with all that money rolling in," Dad said, walking on toward the deep woods. "No reason for us to keep livin' in that old shack me and Daddy built years ago. We'll build us a fifty-room mansion."

I wanted Dad to shut up—to stop talking about his plans for Sartain Woods. It was getting dark now. I wanted to turn around and go back home. I didn't care if we had a Christmas tree.

"Daniel, bring me the saw. I done found us a good one."

I didn't want to go over there, but I did go.

"Look-a-here at the shape on this beauty," Dad said, pointing to a cedar by the path.

"It's taller than the ceiling," I said, trying to imagine the huge tree stuffed into our tiny living room.

"We'll make it fit," Dad said, reaching for the saw. He squatted by the tree and started cutting, then stopped. "You do the honors, son," he said, handing me the saw.

My fingers closed around the handle. The jagged saw

blade stared back at me like the grimacing teeth of a comic book villain.

No way was I cutting this tree. I was out here in the woods with Dad even though it was the last place I wanted to be. But I didn't have to saw anything.

"You started already, Dad. You cut the tree." I held the saw out, hoping he'd take it back.

"Humph," Dad said. His mouth quivered a moment; then he folded his lips into that mean, straight line I knew too well. "What's so hard about cutting a Christmas tree, son?"

I shrugged.

"And how 'bout you wipe that sad-sack expression off your face? It's Christmas, Daniel. You're supposed to be cheerful."

"I don't have anything to be cheerful about, Dad. You know that."

Dad threw his hands up in the air. He turned back to the tree and pointed at the trunk. "All you gotta do is run that little saw back and forth on that tree trunk. Get over here."

"*No.* I'm not cutting anything." I put my lips in a mean, straight line and glared at Dad like I could set him on fire.

Before Dad could say anything else, I opened my fingers and flung that bow saw like a giant Frisbee into the woods.

Dad's eyes widened as he watched the saw slam against a tree trunk, then fall to the ground.

"I was right. You ain't nothing but a chicken scaredy-cat. Can't shoot a rabbit. Can't show holiday cheer. Can't cut a Christmas tree. Can't, can't, can't. You are one messed-up little boy."

Dad spat on the ground. He limped up the path, looking

wild-eyed around the woods until he spotted another cedar, a tiny, sick-looking one.

"Look-a-here," Dad shouted, grabbing the little cedar and ripping it up by its roots. "Don't need a saw . . . or a son to cut a tree. Take this scrawny thing back to your mama. Tell her you can't even cut down a proper Christmas tree. Can you do that, son? Or does that scare you too much?"

I looked at Dad, shaking that tiny cedar tree at me, with those bare roots dropping dirt all over, and I knew right then that he would always be a mean dad. He could stop drinking. Stop smoking. Go to counseling. Whatever he did, my dad would always be mean.

And I would be just like him before long. My lips had learned to fold into that mean, straight line today. And I could feel my own meanness like a growth inside me, getting bigger every day.

"You gonna answer me, son? Or you gonna just stand there like some dumb tree?"

"Humph," I said, grabbing the cedar from Dad's hand. I turned and ran hard as I could toward home.

• • •

"It's beautiful," Mom said when I handed her the tree. She leaned close to the branches and breathed in the cedar smell. "It's kinda little, though. Let's put it on the table in front of the living room windows. Daniel, go up to the attic and get the decorations."

I did as Mom asked, stacking the tubs in my closet to make a plastic staircase, then climbing up into the darkness.

Something different caught my eye when I turned on the light. Over by the attic window, I saw a pile of old army fatigues. When did those move over there? I headed over to investigate. Digging down through the army green shirts and pants, I found my .410.

I pulled my hands away fast, like I'd just touched something hot. Then I plunged my hands back into the clothes and pulled out my shotgun.

"Put that back where you found it," Clay's voice said.

"No way," I said, sighting down the barrel at an old chest by the window. That broken-down piece of furniture already had a hole in one drawer front. I could put another right beside it.

Was the gun loaded? I lowered it, then cocked it open and stared down the barrel. Empty.

"Daniel, hurry up with the decorations, okay, hon? We're ready for the lights. Just bring one of those small strands. It'll go around three or four times."

Mom's voice in my room.

I buried the gun in its hiding place and walked over to the plastic tubs full of decorations.

chaptereighteen

Mom laughed about the scraggly little tree as we strung it with lights and hung ornaments that night. Dad stood in the kitchen and watched us, drinking beer and puffing out clouds of stinking smoke.

Two presents wrapped in happy-looking Santa paper appeared under our tree the next day. My name was on one. I picked up the box and shook it, then slid it back under the tiny tree. For the first time in my life, I didn't care what was in the box.

The next day was Christmas Eve. Mom's oyster stew bubbled in the stockpot that afternoon, sending the strong smell all over the house.

Mom served steaming bowls of stew that night. I made myself look away from Clay's empty place. Made myself stare down at the tiny oyster crackers floating in my bowl. I liked oyster stew, but I couldn't eat much with Clay's place so empty across the table.

Early on Christmas morning, I yawned and stretched, then rolled out of my bed. The cold wooden floor chilled my bare feet as I pulled on jeans and a flannel shirt. Sitting in my desk chair, I put on my heaviest wool socks and my hiking boots.

At the door, I peered up the hallway, listening to Dad's snores. I darted into the bathroom, closing the door quietly behind me. Maybe my bathroom noises wouldn't wake him, I thought as I peed into the toilet bowl, not bothering to lift the seat.

Mom and Dad looked like they were in a deep sleep when I glanced into their room. Mitzi was curled into a tiny sleeping ball of dog at the foot of their bed. She opened one round dog eye and looked at me for a moment before dozing off again.

I watched Mom's arm move over the pillow, her fingertips touching Dad's dirty brown hair. Dad's mouth opened, letting out an animal-like whistling sound from somewhere deep inside his rusty chest.

The living room was dark and it smelled like stale oyster stew mixed with cedar. I flipped on the overhead light. Presents. Nine boxes with cheery Christmas paper and colorful bows. But I didn't need presents anymore. Maybe Mom would give them to the twins when I was gone.

Back in my room, I opened the closet door and hoisted myself into the attic. I pulled the string, turning on the overhead light. Army clothes scattered as I dug until my fingers found the barrel, then the wooden stock of my .410. One of the shirt pockets held the box of cartridges.

I cracked open my shotgun and dropped a slender black cartridge into the barrel. Like Clay had taught me. I snapped the gun shut.

Holding the .410 against my shoulder, feeling the smooth wood press my cheek, I sighted down the barrel at the attic window.

"*Boom,*" I whispered.

I moved closer and closer, trying not to make the attic floorboards squeak, until I stood at the window. Outside I saw the sun rising in the distance, over Sartain Woods. Sunrise colors, deep reds and fiery yellow oranges, spread across the sky. I knew those light streaks were beautiful. But the more I watched them, the grayer they got.

No matter what I did, I would always hurt. Nothing could change that. Not Mrs. Hardy talking to me in her office. Or Mrs. Pettibone giving me a break on my schoolwork. Or Mom nuzzling the top of my head, trying to soothe me with her Soddy-Daisy mountain talk.

Not even Clay's voice in my head could take away my misery. That wasn't really Clay. It was just my mind, trying to bring him back.

Clay wasn't ever coming back.

And that was my fault.

I squinted my eye, using the silver sight-post at the end of the gun barrel to target a squirrel skittering across the porch roof. I cocked back the hammer and squeezed at the trigger, then stopped, thinking about the noise a gunshot would make in the attic.

That would ruin everything.

I walked back across the attic floor with the gun. The door didn't want to budge at first. Finally, I got it open and, cradling my .410, I dropped back down into my closet, trying not to make any noise.

In my room, I raised the window and climbed out, being careful not to jostle the loaded shotgun.

A dog howled in the distance, sounding as sad and mournful as I felt. I headed down the driveway. Then up Mouse Creek Road, across the meadow and into the woods.

My footsteps crunched against the frosty ground as my breaths puffed out clouds in front of me. I made myself walk faster up the path, thinking about what I'd just left behind: the warm house. Mom and Dad. Mitzi. Presents. I hoped my parents would sleep late this morning—hoped they'd enjoy their rest and the peace and quiet before they found me.

How long would it take them to find me?

I stopped at the lake and watched geese move silently across the misty bluish green water. Breathing in the damp smell, I wondered if maybe I should just forget about what I'd decided to do. The shotgun felt heavy in my hands. What would Mom say if I did this terrible thing? And Mrs. Hardy? Nicole and Eric? And most of all, Clay?

"Clay says you don't want to do this, D-Man. Throw that gun in the lake. I wish I'd never given you Pop's .410."

"Me too." I held the shotgun out over the water, feeling my hands tremble like I was holding something that weighed a million pounds. Grimacing, I tried to force my fingers to let go.

"Let it go, D-Man. Open those fingers and let it go," Clay

pleaded. *"Go back home and open your presents. You'll feel better then."*

"No!" I shouted, making geese squawk and scatter. I'd made up my mind and I wasn't going to change it now. I was tired. Tired of trying to feel better. Tired of the guilt. And most of all, I couldn't stand the meanness growing inside me, hurting more every day, turning me into a Dad-like monster.

How could I go on, feeling like a murderer instead of a regular kid? I was always going to be a chicken scaredy-cat. A monster worse than any villain in my comic books. That boy who shot his uncle.

But the worst thing was, I didn't have Uncle Clay anymore. I missed him so much. He wasn't ever coming back and that was all my fault. My fault. I didn't deserve to be in this world.

I trudged around the lake, back onto the path, and headed past the chimney of the old cabin. Past the place where Dad had ripped the little cedar from the ground. I stopped and looked at the raw earth and bits of root around the hole.

Clutching the .410 tighter, I walked on through the woods until I reached the spot where Clay had gone down. I knew this was the place because the straw was really thick here, like someone had trucked in a whole fresh load and dumped it on the ground to cover up what I had done to Clay.

I propped my gun against a tree and stretched out on the prickly pine straw, looking up into the treetops, watching them sway back and forth in the cold morning breeze.

The tree branches made those eerie whispering sounds

as they moved. And all around me, I smelled the earth and I felt Clay there. His eyes closed. His body still. His blood, thick and red, flowing out of those pellet holes I blew in him with my shotgun.

I was going to bleed . . . and I didn't care.

I stayed there a long time with my eyes closed and my body still, listening to bird music in the trees. Feeling the air move against my face. Breathing in those familiar woodsy smells of trees and earth and animals. Thinking about that morning in the woods with Clay.

Mom would get up soon. She'd roll out of bed with Mitzi right behind her. Today was Friday. She'd pull on her jeans and T-shirt and slide her feet into her pink bedroom slippers and pad into the bathroom. She'd fuss about the mess I'd left on the toilet seat, but she wouldn't bother me about it. Not on Christmas morning.

In the kitchen, she'd make pecan pancakes. She'd mix the buckwheat batter and drop in pecan halves. Spoon pancake-sized circles into the sizzling iron skillet, never guessing that I wasn't safe in my bed.

Dad would cough and sputter and reach for his pack of cigarettes before he got up. He'd stumble into the bathroom smelling like nasty tobacco smoke, and he'd wet the seat Mom had just cleaned.

In the kitchen, Dad would drop into a chair and light another cigarette, listening to Mom call me for breakfast. "That boy oughta be in the living room by now, tearing into his presents," he'd say.

When I didn't show up, Dad would yell, "Daniel, get in here now or I'm gonna eat up all your pancakes."

Mom would shake her head and give Dad a disgusted look as she slid my breakfast into the oven so it would stay warm.

How long would it take them to notice I was gone? Mom's agonized look flashed into my mind. And Dad's shocked face. I saw Clay's face, too. Eyes open, not seeing a thing.

"Stop thinking," I told myself, opening my eyes, squinting at my .410. "It's time to take your shot."

I got up and walked to the tree, feeling my legs tremble with every step. I grabbed the gun and stretched my arms out as far as they'd go, maneuvering the shotgun around until the barrel pressed against my forehead.

Tears stung my eyes as I cocked the hammer and pushed my thumb against the trigger, trying not to think . . . or hurt anymore.

chapternineteen

"What are you doing, D-Man?" Clay's loud voice in my head startled me. I looked around. He sounded so real, like he was here in the woods.

I inhaled, filling my lungs with pine-scented air, then pressed the cold gun barrel back against my forehead, pushing my thumb against the trigger.

Clay was just an imaginary voice in my head. I didn't have to listen to him. This was my shot. I could do it. I could push the trigger with my thumb. I could—

"No way are you going to shoot yourself."

Clay's voice again. Clear and strong. Sounding like it was right beside me.

I lowered the gun and surveyed the woods, studying the trees, the bushes, looking up and down the path.

I was alone. No sign of Clay anywhere. But I felt him all

around me and I heard him breathing in the trees overhead. *Whoosh. Whoosh.* That was the sound of life.

"You ever going to answer my question? What are you doing, D-Man?"

"I'm . . . I'm . . . shooting my gun." I raised the .410 again, ramming the barrel hard against my forehead, feeling the cold metal press into my skin, putting my thumb back against the trigger. "You wanted me to shoot my gun. I'm taking my shot now. And your voice in my head's not going to stop me."

"Didn't I tell you never to point your gun at a human being?"

"A human being?" I sighed and lowered the shotgun. At the moment, I didn't feel much like a human being. I felt like a human being killer. A stupid boy who had shot his uncle. Dead. I might hear his voice in my head, but Clayton Eugene Sartain was dead. Dead and buried in the family graveyard.

"Listen to me, D-Man. This isn't your shot. You don't wanna shoot your gun now. Not this way. That shot you fired? The one that got me? That was an accident. You were just a beginner that day, on your very first hunt. You didn't mean for that gun to go off."

"I was careless. I wasn't paying attention to the gun when I started getting up."

I glanced at the shotgun in my hands. "I'm afraid I'm going to end up like Dad. My mouth is making that line now. And sometimes I feel mean and hateful inside."

"You? Like Ray? That's the craziest thing I've ever heard come out of your mouth, D-Man. You will never be like Ray.

Never in a million years. You aren't even made out of the same stuff."

"But what I did, that was worse than Dad being the driver when Granddaddy and Grandmama got killed."

"Those were both accidents, D-Man. Your gun fired by mistake and one of those little pellets from the cartridge entered my heart and ended my life. That wasn't worse than Ray swerving and hitting a tree and killing Mama and Daddy."

"I can't even look anybody in the eye now. Dad pretends he's better but I don't think he is. Mom cries a lot when she thinks I can't hear her. The kids at school think I'm some kind of freak. Even Nicole and Eric don't know how to talk to me anymore. Mrs. Hardy tried to help me, but I'm never going to be me again. I just want all this to end—"

"For God's sake, you don't wanna shoot yourself this beautiful Christmas morning any more than I wanna be dead, D-Man."

"Yes I do." I raised the .410 again, gripping it hard with my cold, shaking hands. I rammed the barrel against my forehead. Closing my eyes, I moved my trembling thumb against the trigger.

"Remember all those things Mrs. Hardy told you about death? About how everybody's gonna die?"

"Yeah." A ragged sob shook my chest as I thought about the dead ladybug on the table. And how that same thing was going to happen to everyone.

"This isn't your time. When somebody you love dies, you don't follow them. You keep on going, for them and for yourself. You walk where they can't walk anymore. Feel what they can't

feel. Do all the things they can't do. You live for them, Daniel, as well as yourself."

"I can't . . ." I felt the bitter taste of bile bubbling up my throat. I choked it back down and flexed my thumb against the trigger.

"This is your chance, Daniel. Forget about comic book characters. D-Man was just a nickname I made up when we were playing football. He was a character, like Superman and Spider-Man and the Masked Avenger. D-Man was never real.

"But Daniel is real. He is strong and powerful. Daniel can get through this and go on to live his life, for both of us. I know you can do that, Daniel. I know."

I flexed my thumb against the trigger, then stopped as a great gust of wind moved the tree branches all around me. *Whoosh. Whoosh.* The sounds of breathing. Cold air against my face. The smells of earth and pine.

Clay was right. I could be Daniel now. Strong as D-Man, but not a superhero. A boy. A living, breathing boy who is not afraid to go on. I wanted to be like Clay that day I followed him into the woods. I could still be like Clay . . . for the rest of my life . . . if I didn't do this terrible thing . . . if I didn't shoot my .410.

I felt something inside me crumble. Sadness. Guilt. Fear. All those horrible, scary feelings that had filled me since the day Clay and I went rabbit hunting. And in place of all that painful stuff, Clay's words were growing. His words about not giving up. Keeping on. Walking where he couldn't walk anymore, for both of us.

I looked at my thumb twitching against the trigger. Inhaling a deep breath, I felt my blood, Sartain mixed with

Russell—thick and warm, rushing through my veins. Felt my Clay-like muscles budge against my shirtsleeves. Felt all my Daniel powers energize me as my arms lifted high as they could go and heaved that gun into the bushes.

Boom! The gun went off when it landed, shattering the morning stillness, making birds go crazy with frightened squawks and a whooshing of wings as they flew away.

chaptertwenty

I ran through the woods with the burnt gunpowder smell in my nose, thinking about those warm pecan pancakes I hoped Mom had waiting for me in the oven. And the presents under our tiny tree—what would I find in those boxes? I needed one of Mom's hugs, too—the soft kind only Mom could give.

The lake, the woods—everything blurred together as I ran on, crossing the meadow and sprinting down Mouse Creek Road toward our house.

I stopped about midway up the driveway, holding my side, trying to catch my breath. Mr. Hooper's pickup was parked by our front porch. He and Dad were standing by the open tailgate. The way their heads moved and Dad's hands jerked this way and that, I could tell they were arguing about something. Mom stood near Dad, twisting a dish towel in her hands.

I heard them before I saw them: two young beagles dragging their leashes, barking and running around our yard, wagging their tails.

One of the dogs almost knocked me over as he jumped against me, licking my face with his rough, wet tongue. He smelled doggy as he pushed his warm body against me, nuzzling my arm.

I caught hold of the pup. This was my dog, the one Clay had told me about the day we went rabbit hunting. He was perfect. Sturdy and strong with short white fur and brown and black patches. And a white-tipped tail and dark, soulful beagle eyes.

The other dog, the one jumping up on Dad, looked almost the same. Clay would have loved that beagle, I thought, watching Dad push him away.

"I wanted to say something about these dogs at the funeral, but it didn't seem like the right time," Mr. Hooper said. "All the other puppies got adopted a while back. I've been keeping these two for you folks. Christmas day seemed like the right time to bring 'em over."

"Nobody asked you to bring these hounds over here today, Frank. You think I got money to pay you?" Dad spat on the ground beside Mr. Hooper's truck and glared at our neighbor.

"Clay told me to bring 'em to his cabin when they were ready to leave their mama, Ray. They're past ready, and I can't deliver them to Clay, now can I? So I brought them to you. He already paid. Cash. Anyway, one of the dogs belongs to Daniel."

Mr. Hooper looked at me and grinned. "Merry Christmas, boy."

Dad shook his head and pushed away the dog trying to lick his hand. "How much my brother give you?"

"Fifty apiece. That mostly covered the shots and worming," Mr. Hooper said, frowning.

"How 'bout you give me a refund? And take these stinking dogs back where they came from. We already got one dog and that's one more than I want."

"You're not serious," Mr. Hooper said. "I figured you'd be glad to see these dogs today. Clay wanted Daniel to have one, you know. It was a nice thing he did, buying a dog for that boy. He needs a pet after what he's been through. I bet Dan would say this is the best Christmas present he ever got."

"Frank's right," Mom said, putting her hand on Dad's arm. "Look at how much he loves these dogs already. He'll be heartbroken if you don't let him keep at least one."

Dad's face darkened as he looked at me, then looked at the dogs nuzzling against me, like he was inspecting them, trying to decide if they were good dogs.

I squatted and pulled one of the dogs close, feeling puppy breath warm on my face as I rubbed the white fur on his belly. The pup twisted around and licked my face all over, making me smell like a beagle.

"His name is Lightning, Dad," I said, rubbing my nose against the dog, feeling his whiskers brush my cheek. "Like that dog you used to have?"

"Humph," Dad said. He looked at Mom, then turned to Mr. Hooper and said, "Take 'em back."

"*Ray!*" Mom took her hand off Dad's arm. She stared hard at him, like she could change his mind with a strong enough look.

The other beagle brushed up against me then, trying to get between me and Lightning, like he was jealous. I made room for him and tried to hold both squirming dogs back so they wouldn't run over to Dad.

Clay's dog broke loose. Before I could stop him, he jumped up in Dad's face.

"Get away!" Dad yelled, pushing the dog to the ground, making him whimper.

"Clay was going to name him Caesar, Dad," I said, hoping Dad would like the dog better if he knew his name. Maybe he'd change his mind about sending the dogs back.

Dad reached out his hand toward Caesar's head, then pulled it back when the dog nipped at him.

"Clay called Caesar one tough dog's name," I said. And then I waited for Dad to think about that. Didn't Dad have any decent feelings in him at all? He had to let me keep the dogs.

Dad just stood there, looking like he was holding back something painful inside as he stared at Clay's dog.

"If anybody needs a dog, you do, Dad," I blurted.

"Daniel's right, Ray," Mom said. "Let's keep both dogs. Clay would want us to do that."

Dad drew his lips up into that mean line. He leaned close to Caesar and extended his tobacco-stained fingers toward the beagle's head.

Just before his hand touched the dog's brown and white fur, Dad jerked it away. "Nope. We ain't taking on these dogs. Put 'em back in the truck, Frank."

"You're making a mistake," Mr. Hooper said, rounding up the dogs and loading them into the truck bed.

Mr. Hooper slammed the tailgate. He pulled down the camper top and twisted the knob.

"You know, Ray, I was good buddies with your daddy," Mr. Hooper said, turning around and looking at Dad. "If he was here today, he wouldn't let anybody take his grandson's dog away."

Dad glared at Mr. Hooper. "You don't know what my daddy would say. Get away from here, Frank. Take the dogs." Dad slapped the camper top window with his hand, setting off a round of barking.

"Whatever you say," Mr. Hooper said, climbing into his pickup. "If you change your mind, let me know. I'll hang on to 'em awhile."

I watched Old Man Hooper's truck wobble down our long driveway and I wanted to run after those dogs.

"Ray, why didn't you let Daniel have at least one beagle? That's what Clay wanted—"

"Shut up, Melissa," Dad said.

When I turned back around, Dad was balling his fist at Mom.

I wasn't going to let Dad have his way this time. Clay wouldn't let his brother get away with this.

"Quit talking mean to Mom, Dad!" I shouted, balling my fist and shaking it in his direction.

"What'd you say to me, son?" Dad looked at me with his hateful eyes. He walked closer with his fist ready for action.

"Daniel, let's go in the house," Mom said, taking my arm and pulling me toward the porch.

"No!" I felt adrenaline pumping as I glared back at Dad. "You can't even pet a dog, Dad. Or tell me you're sorry you didn't come hunting with us that day when Clay got killed. Don't you care about anything other than your beer and those nasty cigarettes?"

Dad lowered his hand. He shook a cigarette from the pack in his shirt pocket and lit it. He inhaled, then puffed a blue-gray cloud of smoke into the air between us, like he was daring me to do something about it.

"You go, Dad!" I shouted. "We don't want to keep you. Go on. Get out of here."

"Let me tell you something, boy," he said, getting right up in my face. "This is my house. And this land all around us—up Mouse Creek Road and all the way to Hooper Gap—it's all mine. I ain't going nowhere."

chaptertwenty-one

That night I lay in my bed and stared out the window at the darkness, thinking about those dogs Dad had sent back with Mr. Hooper. Lightning would be here right now, his tail thumping on the covers, if Dad had let me have him. Caesar would be here, too.

I was going to tell Mrs. Hardy what Dad had done today. Maybe when I went back to school after the holidays I'd tell her every mean thing he'd ever done. I'd have to tell her what I'd almost done in the woods today, too. How I'd held that gun one more time and how close I'd come to firing it.

I knew now that shooting my gun that way would have proved that I was a chicken scaredy-cat, like Dad said. Not taking my shot, throwing that gun away . . . that took guts.

Mrs. Hardy would be glad I didn't take my shot. She'd sit at the octagonal table, in one of those little blue chairs, and we'd talk it through.

And I could stay there in her turquoise room as long as I wanted, staring at that clay flower. She'd probably let me paint it all the way to the edges if I wanted to. And I wanted to.

I was thinking about how good that paint was going to look when I heard steps in the hall. My doorknob twisted, then stopped.

Closing my eyes, I pretended I was in a deep sleep, making my breaths go in and out in a regular rhythm.

The doorknob twisted again and the door squeaked open. Heavy footsteps walked into my room.

I smelled Dad's tobacco stench when he sat on my bed, making the mattress wobble as he settled himself near me. Not touching, but so close I could feel him there.

Dad sighed. He coughed deep in his chest and moved a little on the bed, making the mattress crackle, like he wanted to wake me.

Still, I kept my eyes closed tight. I didn't have to open my eyes for Dad. Why was he here? I didn't have any use for him and he didn't have any business keeping me from sleeping.

"Daniel?" Dad said my name real soft. "You don't have to open your eyes. Just listen to me."

What could Dad possibly say that I wanted to hear? I wanted him off my bed. Out of my room. Out of my life. I didn't need him.

Dad coughed again and tried to clear his throat. The sound went on for a long time, like he couldn't get rid of what was bothering him.

"I got something to tell you, son. I'm . . . leaving. Can't

stop drinking by myself. So I'm going to Augusta . . . to this treatment center for some help. That counselor I been seeing . . . he said it'd be the best thing to do. Your mama . . . she agrees."

Dad was going away? I opened my eyes and looked up at him. He was just a shadow there on my bed, with his face almost hidden in the darkness. But I could make out his lips and they were not a mean straight line.

Dad patted my arm, then let his big, rough hand slide down until it covered mine.

"Shoulda let you keep them dogs. And I'm sorry I didn't go hunting with you and Clay. Shoulda been there that day, Daniel. But I thought Clay was enough for you. He made a real good daddy, didn't he? I'm glad you had him—glad we all had him."

Dad got up. He leaned over and ruffled my hair, then turned and walked out of my room.

For a long time, I lay there in my bed, thinking about what Dad had said. As far back as I could remember, I'd never heard Dad say he was sorry about anything. The closest he'd ever come was that day he chased me into Clay's cabin and told me about his guilt over that car wreck on Hooper Gap. I'd never heard him call Clay a daddy, either, but I guess that was what my uncle was.

I didn't believe Dad was really going anywhere.

The sound of his pickup truck cranking changed my mind. I rolled out of bed as he gunned the engine, and I ran to the living room window. The hairs on the back of my neck prickled as I watched those two glowing taillights float down our rutted driveway.

"It's okay, Daniel," Mom said, coming up behind me and curling her arms around my shoulders. "He needs to go."

We watched Dad's truck turn onto Mouse Creek Road. My heart started beating really hard then. And I felt little sweat beads pop out on my face. I'd wanted Dad to go—told him to go. But now that he was gone I felt sadness spreading over me and I didn't know why.

Mom's breathing sounds got louder. I felt her arms tighten around me like she didn't ever want to let go as the truck taillights faded out of sight.

"Is he coming back?"

Mom didn't answer. Her arms around me trembled.

"Mom? How long does that treatment in Augusta take?"

Mom propped her chin against my head and let out a long sigh. "Do you want him to come back?"

I wasn't expecting Mom to ask me that question. Like I was a grown-up and I had a say in a decision like that. I didn't know the answer to Mom's question as I stared out the window, thinking about Dad driving up the road toward Newtonville. Then on to Augusta by himself.

Mom sighed, puffing my hair with her warm breath. "What would you think if your dad never came back?"

She waited for my answer, squeezing me harder, rocking us back and forth as we stared through the window at the darkness.

For a long time, I didn't answer. I stood there imagining my life without Dad. No clouds of cigarette smoke. No pops of beer-can tops. No mean looks and hurting words.

I was learning to live without Clay. Maybe I could do without Dad. But I wasn't sure I wanted to. I needed a dad. I wanted them to help him in Augusta. Make him stop drinking and smoking. Make him talk nicer. Make him want to come home and be my dad. Could they do that at the treatment center? Could anybody do that?

"I reckon I'd miss him very much if he never came back," Mom said in a soft voice. "But I would hate him forever if he came back the same. If he didn't change."

I turned then and looked at Mom. At her lips trembling and those tiny trails of mascara dripping down her scared face.

"I didn't mean what I said, Mom. When Dad made Mr. Hooper take back the dogs. When I told him to go. He just made me so mad."

"Oh, Daniel," Mom said. She brushed the hair out of my face and touched my chin with her fingertip. "You got to your daddy today. Made him think. Showed him how he looks to you. Told him what he needed to hear. You don't have to apologize for that."

Mom walked me back to my room with her arm draped across my shoulder. I crawled into my bed and she pulled the quilt over me and tucked it around my shoulders.

"We never opened our presents," Mom said. She leaned over and kissed my forehead. "We'll do that after breakfast. I know you're gonna like what you get."

"Will you make pecan pancakes for breakfast?" I asked, thinking about those pancakes I had missed while I was out in the woods.

"Of course," Mom said. "And Mr. Hooper is joining us."

I sat up in bed. "Mr. Hooper's eating pancakes with us?"

Mom smiled. "I told him we'd have plenty. Your dad called him before he left. Frank's bringing the dogs back."

"Dad called Mr. Hooper?"

Mom nodded.

"Both of 'em? Mr. Hooper's bringing both beagles?"

"Yes, hon. We'd better get some sleep now. Frank's going to help us build a dog pen tomorrow. Mitzi wouldn't take too kindly to two frisky beagles moving into the house, now would she?"

I grinned at Mom. "She'd probably go into one of her shaking fits and pass out," I said.

"And let's not even think about what the beagles would do then," Mom said.

I listened to Mom's footsteps as she walked down the hall to her room. Tomorrow, after we ate pecan pancakes and built that dog pen, maybe I'd finish reading the "Mild-Mannered Superman" comic.

And after that, I'd take Lightning and Caesar for a walk through the woods to the lake. And I'd tell them all about Clay, and how we were walking for him. And walking for us, too.

lettertothereader

Dear Reader,

I was born in Athens, Georgia, a Southern town that now numbers about 112,000 people and is sixty-five miles from Atlanta. Athens is home to the University of Georgia, the first state-chartered land-grant university; a tree that owns itself; and the world's only double-barreled cannon. My hometown is also known for a thriving music scene that spawned rock groups including R.E.M., the B-52's, and Widespread Panic.

But if you drive just a few miles outside the Athens city limits, you will find yourself in the rural South, surrounded by pine trees and pickup trucks. In this paradise of undeveloped, wooded land dotted by tiny towns such as Winterville, where I've lived for more than fifteen years, the tradition of hunting is still passed down from generation to generation in many families.

Though our pioneer ancestors depended on

firearms and hunting skills for survival, most Georgians today consider hunting a sport. Deer, rabbit, and other wild game are eaten, but for most families, hunting is not their primary source of meat.

So why do we hunt? For many reasons. Some hunters believe that wild game is healthier than the meat we find in today's grocery stores. Department of Natural Resources rangers tell us that hunting is a conservation tool of healthy herd management. For some, hunting is an enjoyable way to spend time outdoors with family and friends.

When this book was written, approximately 12.5 million Americans hunted. That number is declining each year, and experts predict that it will decline by half during the next twenty years. Reasons for this decline include the development of rural land, which leaves fewer areas for hunting, and the increased number of parents who do not hunt or pass the tradition to the next generation. Also, more children today live in urban areas, where video games and other distractions keep them indoors.

Some people do not believe in hunting wild animals—or even in owning guns. There are organizations devoted to eradicating gun ownership and the killing of animals. But hunters and nonhunters alike agree that handling firearms can be dangerous, especially for inexperienced hunters like Daniel Sartain.

In 1992, Clay would have had a hunting license. Daniel, as a hunter under age sixteen, would not have been required to buy a license. Today, hunters in Georgia and many other states must complete a hunter safety course before receiving a hunting license. They are also required to wear "hunter orange" while hunting.

Here is something you should know: In writing this book, it was not my intention either to advocate the hunting and killing of wild animals or to discourage such activity. While I am not a hunter myself, I can trace my family back to pioneer Georgians who settled, hunted, and survived on rural lands in Oglethorpe and Wilkes counties as early as the 1700s. If they hadn't been hunters, I wouldn't be here today. At the same time, I could never shoot an animal and then consume its flesh.

But what about you? If you live in a rural area, you may already be a hunter. City dwellers who come from a family that doesn't hunt may never have considered such an activity. I urge you to think about this issue. Talk to your family and find out how they feel. Go to the library and read about hunting and guns. If you decide to hunt with a firearm, make sure you follow all safety rules and regulations.

Here is something else you should know: Though Daniel's story is fictional, the idea for this story came from events in the life of a real boy and his uncle. If I told you their story, none of the details would exactly match the story of Daniel and his uncle Clay. But the essence of that real boy's story is here, between the pages of this book. Like Daniel, he had to learn to live with what he'd done for the rest of his life. And he did live until his early sixties, contributing much to his family and community until his own untimely death in a car accident.

There is another real uncle hidden in this story as well. The spirit and love of my own uncle, Terry Bailey, floats through this story like a ghost. He died at age thirty-four, but just as Uncle Clay lives on in Daniel, my uncle lives on through me and my story.

Another thing you should know: Suicide may seem like an unlikely choice for Daniel, but a thousand kids in the United States commit suicide every year. If you or someone you know is contemplating suicide, please get help. Talk to your mom, dad, teacher, or school counselor. You can also call the National Suicide Prevention Lifeline, 1-800-273-TALK. Trained counselors are available at that number twenty-four hours a day, seven days a week.

You may be wondering why Daniel didn't pull out a cell phone and call for help after the hunting accident in the woods. Why did Mr. Hooper call for help on his handheld ham radio instead of using a cell phone? The answer is simple. In 1992, the year in which this story takes place, only one percent of the world's population owned a cell phone. And even for those who had such a gadget, coverage would be rare, especially in a rural area like Newtonville.

Can you imagine our world without cell phones? How about a world without the Internet and personal computers in many homes? The World Wide

Web was launched to the public on August 6, 1991, but very few people had access to the Internet at the time this story takes place. Imagine how different your life would be if you lived without the technology many of us take for granted, like iPods, HDTVs, and text messaging.

After reading Daniel's story, I want you to remember this: Guns are dangerous; handle them with care, if you handle them at all. And if you or someone you know so much as mentions suicide, get help.

And above all, I want you to know that if a loved one dies, you can go on.

—Donny Bailey Seagraves

kidsandguns: thestatistics

Fifteen children are killed with guns
each day in the United States.

Firearms are the second leading cause of death
of children and young adults between the ages
of one and twenty-four.

Suicide is the third leading cause of
death of children ages ten through fourteen.

Every nine hours, a child or teen is
killed by a firearm-related accident or suicide.

On average in each of the past ten years, more than
1,000 kids committed suicide with a firearm;
105 were under fifteen years old.

The rate of firearm deaths of children under fourteen
years old is nearly twelve times as high in the

United States as in twenty-five other
industrialized countries combined.

Some 1.2 million American latchkey children
come home each school day to a house
in which there is a gun.

Every day, 135,000 American children
bring guns to school.

**Sources of the above statistics and
for more information:**

American Foundation for Suicide Prevention
www.afsp.org

Association of Suicidology
www.suicidology.org

Brady Campaign to Prevent Gun Violence
(formerly the Center to Prevent Handgun Violence)
www.bradycampaign.org

Centers for Disease Control and Prevention
(CDC–WISQARS)
www.cdc.gov

Children's Defense Fund
www.childrensdefense.org

Common Sense About Kids and Guns
www.kidsandguns.org

Pediatrics for Parents
www.pedsforparents.com

acknowledgments

I am deeply thankful to the following: My editor, Michelle Poploff, for giving me a chance to tell this story and for her careful, thoughtful editing. Orly Henry, Michelle's assistant, for her helpful input. My husband, Phillip Seagraves, and my children, Greg and Jenny Seagraves, for their longtime love and support. My Powersurge writers' group members, Cindy Crain, Jacqueline Elsner, Lola Finn, Lori Hammer, Gail Karwoski, Judy McSpadden, Sharon Wright Mitchell, Muriel Pritchett, Bettye Stroud, Susan Vizurraga, and Amy Winders, for literary inspiration plus endless critiques.

Also Harriette Austin, Mary Ann Coleman, Rosemary Daniell, Gene Fehler, Peggy Hancock, Lee Hartle, Nick Jenkins, Becky Kelley, Kathleen McGuire, Darcy Pattison, Eric Pozen, Joseph Sanger, Doris Buchanan Smith, Pat Thruston, and Philip Lee Williams. Each one of you contributed in your own way.

And finally, many, many thanks to Jo Kittinger, Donna Bowman, and everyone in the Southern Breeze Region of SCBWI, for all you do to help members like me reach publication.

abouttheauthor

Donny Bailey Seagraves is a native of Athens, Georgia. She lives in the nearby small town of Winterville with her husband, Phillip. They are the parents of grown twins, Greg and Jenny. Donny studied journalism at the University of Georgia, was a newspaper columnist for seven years, and has published fiction and nonfiction in many regional and national publications, including *Athens Magazine* and the *Chicago Tribune*. When not reading, writing, or collecting books, Donny enjoys walking in the rural areas around her home, including her own front-yard woods. *Gone from These Woods* is her debut novel. For more information, visit donnyseagraves.com.